THE GARDEN SURPRISES

Philosophical Gardening
or Gardening Philosophy?

Rosi MorganBarry

Front cover photograph: Donald Monk

ISBN 1 85852 102 5

CONTENTS

INTRODUCTION

This is not a gardening book. There are plenty of how-to-do-it books, beautifully written and superbly illustrated by experts who have knowledge, experience, authority and the paper qualifications to prove it; one more by an amateur would be not only superfluous but presumptuous. My own qualification is in quite a different area, but my grandfather was a professional gardener; and my father, mother, aunts, uncles and cousins have all passed on their love of plants in and out of the garden. I acknowledge that love with gratitude, but am dubious about whether I can claim equal expertise.

Neither is it a book on philosophy. I have a respect bordering on reverence for philosophers, never having quite rid myself of the notion that if a book is incomprehensible it must therefore be extremely clever. And most philosophy books (with some notable exceptions) are incomprehensible. But the garden has very often provided inspiration which, as a Methodist local preacher, I have been able to use in illustration of some of life's truths and conundrums. Some of them are presented here.

My own gardens have been places where I go to dig, plant, weed and prune, to work, think, plan, pray and shape ideas from nebulous nothings into words, poems, sermons and stories. They have been places to flee to in times of trouble; they have been places where I can dance and sing (but only when the neighbours are out!) in the good times and at other times they have been places of shelter, harbour, refuge and escape.

The thoughts engendered by the particular garden I had when I wrote this owe much to conversations with my neighbours – especially with one neighbour who is a natural-born philosopher, garden lover, musician, artist, mechanic and humorist. He deserves a chapter all to himself, and if I feel I can do him justice, he shall have one. Meanwhile, the garden tells its own parables – for those who have ears to hear. All I have done is to write them down.

1

❀ ❀ ❀ ❀

KNOW YOUR WEEDS

There is a common assumption, held specifically by those who do little or no gardening, that weeds are pernicious, all-encroaching, invasive nuisances which must be hoed, uprooted and disposed of at all costs, particularly at the cost of one's time and one's back muscles. Some gardeners also hold this point of view, but if you ask them: 'What exactly is a weed, then?' you will get a look of undisguised astonishment that anyone could be so silly as not to know. Indeed, for many gardeners, the distinction between them and the rest of the world is that they (the gardeners) know their weeds from their onions.

Weeds, like people, come in all sizes, types and degrees of personality; there are good weeds, not-so-good weeds and downright bad weeds. They can be shy, assertive or absolutely belligerent, small or large, deep or shallow. Or any combination of the above. Some come and go in a season with a carefree come-today-go-tomorrow approach to life; others cling tenaciously and perennially to one particular patch (usually the bed marked out by the gardener for something special) and refuse all attempts to budge them. And yes, they do have to be dealt with, if you want a garden as opposed to a wilderness. 'But,' you may say, 'I like a wilderness.' I suspect that what you really mean by that is a wild garden or meadow, which is actually a very different thing, and requires a great deal of organising and attention.

To begin to deal with weeds (and people) it is necessary to understand them, and to do that it is necessary to categorise them. So let's start at the bottom with the really aggressive baddies, those which a friend once labelled, with deep feeling, 'horridness weeds'. These include in my garden couch grass, bindweed, stinging nettles, brambles, ground elder and mare's tail (Equisetum arvense). I grew up calling this mare's tail but it is usually referred to as 'field horsetail'. No doubt other people can come up with their own list of horridnesses. They usually have root systems that a spy network would do well to emulate: creeping, branching and connecting for miles, out of sight and secretive. For example, there is the thick, white, wide-spreading, wiggly root-system of bindweed, or the sandy-yellow, hairy, tangly strands of stinging nettle roots. Dig them out year after year; back they come year after year. Because however carefully you dig, there's always a tiny bit of root left that will gleefully start growing fast; the bit that hides itself under the spade, or that wiggles further down than you happen to be digging. And, of course, they inevitably sneak under the fence into your neighbour's garden, which will annoy him very much indeed if he is a careful gardener, and annoy you very much indeed if he is not. Having sneakily crept out of your reach, they will just as sneakily creep back again when you're not looking. So, resign yourself to possibly winning the battle against them each season, but don't deceive yourself into thinking you can win the war.

Actually, digressing for a moment, I did once hear a tale from a lady who won the war against couch grass. Mind you, she was a professional gardener, working in the beautiful gardens of Tresco in the Scilly Isles. She had been set to dig and clear a new patch of weedy wilderness in the first stage of its transformation into a garden, and she battled right stoutly with the couch grass – for days. Down and down she dug, several feet down as well as across the patch, until she stood in a trench up to her knees. Still the couch-grass roots went down, and down she went after them until – she unearthed a human skeleton, buried unboxed, with a bullet hole in its skull and couch grass roots winding it around like a shroud. Up it all came, roots, bones and all. Who the unlucky fellow was no-one ever knew, but to this day (she said) there is not a sign of couch-grass in that particular patch of the Tresco gardens.

My own special battle is against mare's tail, which has developed a strong liking for my strawberry patch. (To do it justice, it was there first.) This particular baddie thinks – maybe rightly – that it has relations in Australia, and that the quickest way to visit them is to grow straight down. It is also underhanded in that these long down-thrusting roots are black, unlike bindweed or nettles whose roots do at least show up clearly against freshly turned soil. It dies right down in winter, so that when you come to dig the ground over in spring, a small, easily overlooked, brownish mare's-tail head can be found to be attached to a yards-long black root.

Very easy to miss altogether until the wretched thing has grown into a green spear, but by that time it, and all its numerous friends and relations have spiked their way up through a patch of carefully planted strawberry plants.

Now I'm not saying that these weedy horridnesses do not have their place in The Grand Design; indeed many cheerful souls proclaim that: 'A Weed is only a Flower growing in the Wrong Place.' (Most of those who propound this remark are not gardeners.) Still, they do have a point: stinging nettles provide food and shelter for several species of butterfly grubs, and a waving sea of mare's tail fronds can cheer up a dull, dirty railway embankment no end. The bramble has been described by David Attenborough, in his book, *The Secret Life of Plants,* as a most successful plant form, because of its multitudinous small prickles and unendearing habit of arching its stems up-and-over anything growing nearby, end-rooting them into new plants – but it does provides us with scrummy blackberries. The bindweed's flaring white trumpet flowers are truly decorative over an unsightly fence or derelict building. All of these are classified as utter baddies in the garden because of their smothering, all-enveloping nature that will not be defeated. You have to admire their tenacity, but you don't have to allow them to rampage all over your garden.

Another group of weeds are the 'surlies'. They can be either annual or perennial, and include chickweed, shepherd's purse, groundsel, bittercress, dandelions . . . Some of them spread themselves about very readily but can be pulled out by hand relatively easily, if perpetually; others root themselves in inaccessible places. Dandelions, for example, can be trowelled out (rather than having to be spaded out, like the mare's tails) but as like as not they will settle themselves between cracks in the paving, or in the lawn, or will threddle their way out from under the very biggest rock in the rockery.

But memories of blowing dandelion clocks in childhood (thus, of course, helping them to spread far and wide) and trying to catch the drifting fairy seeds, so light that they always eluded sticky little hands, render these particular surlies more acceptable – anywhere but in the garden. They too have their rightful place: gold dandelion flowers, like bright new sovereigns flung by a careless philanthropist into the drabbest of city corners, are a truly cheering sight.

Many weeds fall decisively into the 'flower-in-the-wrong-place' group. They may be invasive or pernicious, but they have a truly redeeming feature which puts them – for me – into the category of 'cheerful weeds'. They include daisies, creeping buttercup, speedwell, scarlet pimpernel and all the various willow-herbs . . . My neighbour-on-one-side, who is a wilderness type of gardener (especially round the edges, where his garden borders mine) also puts forget-me-nots in this weedy category, and indeed they spread themselves about with remarkable abandon. More of them later.

I have various ways of dealing with these cheerful weeds. Daisies-in-the-lawn I flatly refuse to remove – a lawn ought to have daisies – but they are not allowed anywhere else in the garden. My daisies seem to have learned this and are well-behaved enough not even to think of appearing anywhere else. (The only trouble with daisies-in-the-lawn, someone once said to me, is that you have to cut their little heads off every time you mow the grass. It's no good being sentimental about this, although if it really worries you, you can always wait until sundown when the flowers close up – that way they won't see themselves being decapitated. But perhaps that's carrying eccentricity a bit too far . . .)

Buttercups are also allowed, but only under very strict supervision, in the 'wild garden'. As mentioned earlier, this is the carefully maintained meadow garden in which self-sown plants – primroses, foxgloves, bluebells, and others are not only permitted but encouraged. Because it is self-seeded, and allowed to do more or less what it likes, the characteristics of the wild garden vary from year to year. But doing what it likes does not include growing horridness weeds!

Speedwell, scarlet pimpernel and the willow-herbs (I seem to have several varieties of these, from great to rosebay to short-fruited) are permitted to flower wherever they appear, then get whisked out before their seeds set. At least, that's the idea, but they have a tendency to get on with things while I'm out shopping.

If some weeds are flowers in the wrong place, then some flowers fall into the category of 'flowers-that-think-they're-weeds'. Like the domestic cat that goes feral, they think and act like wild . . . but that's quite another story.

It's a great puzzle why some weeds – and some people – seem to want to take over the earth, or at least a particular patch of it, to the detriment of anything and everything else that would like to grow there. Territorial rights seem to be the root (sorry!) cause of disputes, battles and out-and-out wars. Yet, taking a world view, even in the wildest of true wildernesses there is botanic variety; the plants seem to have reached some agreement as to what should grow where, and how much of the good earth can be allotted to any one as opposed to any other. I suspect that in the plant world The Ultimate Gardener has things well in hand.

2

❀ ❀ ❀ ❀

FERAL FLOWERS

My friend Enid once told me of a famous conductor who advised young aspiring conductors to be very careful about how they treated the various sections of the orchestra. One of his most important maxims was:

Never look encouragingly at the brass.

That interesting piece of philosophy can be equally applied to the garden . . .

Forget-me-nots could be included in the brass section in the garden; the flowers might be small, but the plants are bold. Give them an inch and they take over the lot, ousting out everything else, so that you end up with a brass band instead of an orchestra. They disperse themselves about all over the place to form a carpet of soft blue, echoing the colour of the spring sky, which looks quite glorious in late April and into May, but which prevents the growth of anything else through the rest of the year. I think they're beautiful, but I have to try and treat them like cheerful weeds, and whisk them out before the seeds set and disperse. In this I am invariably unsuccessful.

My wilderness neighbour regards them with disfavour for some reason. I found him one day, sitting on an upturned bucket by his pond and looking very gloomy. 'My wife's just bought six packets of forget-me-not seeds,' he said, and made it sound as though the end of the world had come. Some people don't like brass bands either.

There are also various other plants that just happen to like my garden, and will rampage all over it if allowed – thus earning the description of 'feral' flowers. (These are in contrast to true well-behaved garden flowers, which stay tidily in the space allotted to them by the gardener, and wouldn't dream of getting up to any tricks in another bed . . .) *Aquilegia*, also known as Columbine or Granny's Nightcaps, pop up in all sorts of unexpected places. Violets too grow everywhere. Don't believe all that Victorian poetic nonsense about 'the shy, shrinking violet'. They are the cheekiest scallywags I know, and have seeded themselves in all sorts of nooks and crannies: in the herbaceous borders, in the rose garden, under the lavender bush, in among the herbs, even in the lawn. On early summer days, sitting in the garden with some work and a cup of tea, I have *heard* them, popping their tricorn seedpods and shooting out little black seeds far and wide, right under my nose. They seem to know I like them too much to reprove them for their profligate habits; besides I can always pass some of the numerous new plants on to my neighbours-on-the-other-side.

What about *Buddleia*? Also known as the Butterfly bush, it is an alleycat plant that grows cheerfully in all kinds of weedy places: you will find it along railway tracks, in city corners, sticking (sometimes horizontally) out of cracks in an old wall, waving itself about over derelict buildings, flourishing in farmyards especially around the dungheap, and livening up bits of broken brick and rubble on a building site. It can also hobnob with the best of flowers in my garden, without changing its dress; its spires of pinky-purple flowers nod over the fence and mingle cheerfully with the climbing rose on the left and the *Lavatera* on the right.

Feral plants, growing as prolifically as they do, can form a useful foundation for a relatively cheap and trouble-free garden. My friend Merle acquired a demanding job in London, a busy husband, twin boys, an elderly house, and a large expanse of wilderness which had been woefully neglected, all in the space of a few years; some people live their lives in a hurry! She cajoled me into discussing ideas for turning the sorry plot into a garden, not that I needed very much persuasion: I was rewarded by a day of her wonderful cooking. Having steered her away from thoughts of growing the grand exotics that flourish in her native South Africa, our plans revolved around the shrubs, plants and bulbs that flourish in her particular bit of London, and would not therefore need much in the way of cossetting. *Buddleia*, of course, but also spiky, sweet-scented and early-flowering *Mahonia*, *Clematis Montana* to scramble over the fences, white-flowered and red-berried *Cotoneaster*, and the ubiquitous and inevitable daffodils, forget-me-nots, the *Saxifrage* aptly named 'London Pride' and Michaelmas daisies, to name but a few.

The interesting thing about feral plants is that they often revert to their wild form, even after much careful attention from the gardener. I have a thornless blackberry, given to me by my sister-in-law Mary, which was doing very-nicely-thank-you, until it began to come under the wild influence of the bramble on my neighbour's side of the fence. (My neighbour has several brambles all along his fence; they intrude themselves through the palings but with not a berry in sight. I consider this most unfair: I send roses and honeysuckle over the fence to his side, and get brambles, stinging nettles, bindweed and various other horridnesses in return!)

I have sternly pointed out to my domestic blackberry the outrageous behaviour of the bramble; I have discoursed on its profligate habits, and on all the attendant disadvantages of such an alliance. I have told it that nicely-brought-up plants don't go rampaging about, and that if they associate with wild types they will grow prickles. Alas, my words have fallen on deaf leaves; I am embarrassed to report that the two plants have combined themselves all over the fence, and I now cannot tell which is which. To add insult to injury, the blackberry crop over the past few years has steadily declined in quality and quantity. Fruits of a *mésalliance* indeed!

What more can anyone do? Plants, like children, sometimes have to be left to do their own thing. To take a walk on the wild side, pick the wild fruit, sow their wild oats, grow prickles and in turn get scratched by life's thorns. All the gardener, or a parent, can do is to prune and advise, nourish and cherish, disentangle and dissuade. A man had two sons, and the younger squandered all his means in dissolute living. He spent all he had, and then came to his senses. He went home to his father, who welcomed him home with feasting and festivity. There is space in the garden for all, including the feral plants – provided that they keep to their space.

3

❀ ❀ ❀ ❀

EARLY SPRING DAYS

One February, I took a day off to work at home. But, in spite of having several pieces of work to complete, I was tempted away from the computer and out into the garden by as beguiling a sun as ever shone at any time of year, let alone early in February. The sky was pellucid blue and the breeze a fresh but erratic south-westerly. Up and down the street, windows were flung open, bedlinen and towels washed and hung outside to dry for the first time this year. They were brought indoors in the late afternoon, cold, still faintly dampish, but smelling sweetly of fresh air and wind.

I resolved to spend the morning in the garden – and to be back at my desk in the afternoon, but the hours stretched on to sundown and still I worked. There was so much to be done: many jobs which, for one reason or another (but chiefly due to my own inefficiency) had been left over from last autumn's put-the-garden-to-bed days.

Pruning away the dead stalks of the late-flowering *Sedum* 'Autumn Joy', the Lemon Balm and the irises to let through young growth, I admired the cup-curled leaf-rosettes of the *Sedum* which held rain-water in shining pearly globules. Pulling away the dried montbretia leaves from a large clump by the garden shed I found a resident Mr Toad, cold and torpid in hibernation. I watched the almost imperceptible movement of his sides as he breathed long, slow, shallow breaths. Then I covered him up again and left him to have his sleep out, to conserve his energy so that he can help control next year's slug population. Later, the *Montbretia* growth under the cypress tree yielded a small green frog. He was awake, and startled, but not awake enough to leap high or far. I persuaded him on to my hand and slipped him back into the undergrowth, feeling he was a good excuse to leave that particular spot untouched.

It was too early to prune the roses, but I tidied them a little and cleared some of the underplanted Creeping Jenny from around their boles.   A robin came to perch close by on the fence, announcing his presence with a little trill of song. He was the most raggedy robin I have ever seen; his back and lower chest feathers were all sticking out anyhow, giving him a most bedraggled appearance.   I told him severely he looked as if he had been dragged through a hedge backwards, but he merely flicked his disreputable tail and followed me round the garden, with bright eyes on the lookout for tasty worms. I turned up plenty of those – really big juicy ones, but I rationed Robin's intake because this heavy clay Berkshire soil needs all the wormy activity it can get.

Our two pine trees were still standing, but beginning to show signs of the ill-health which would later necessitate their removal. I cleared away the thick winter fall of pine needles and cones to disclose early violets, primrose buds, tiny miniature daffodils ('February Gold' – my father's favourites) just coming into flower, and one solitary snowdrop. Why is it that though I plant about fifty snowdrop bulbs every year, I manage to get only a few flowers? One or two usually, although one year, they did produce at least six. My friend Mary F. (I have several friends called Mary so have to distinguish them by surname initial) has the same problem, and puts it down to the underground presence of a 'Snowdrop Dragon' which devours the bulbs during the winter. The garden books advise buying them 'in the green' – around the middle of March or early in April when they have finished flowering but you can still see what you are getting. WYSIWYG snowdrops, perhaps?

Along the path, the crocuses had been tempted into flower and were opening up gold, white and purple to the sun. Next-door's little black-and-white cat came prancing down the garden path and, giving in to her insatiable curiosity, squeezed through the fence to see what I was up to, and to lend a paw if she felt like it. Robin beat a hasty retreat to the top of the apple tree and sang defiantly to us, and a blackbird gave his sharp warning call. I had found some ladybirds, inert in winter sleep, although one had woken up and was crawling rather unsteadily over a warm stone, with her six legs not quite co-ordinating with each other. I recited the rhyme about the centipede to her by way of encouragement:

A centipede was happy quite, until a
toad in fun
Said, 'Pray, which leg goes after which?'
Which worked her mind to such a pitch
She lay distracted in a ditch
Considering how to run!

But it did not seem to improve her performance. Neither was she helped by the cat, who decided that this was where she could offer a helping paw and who tried to make her go faster by patting her. The poor creature was rather overwhelmed by this treatment and I had to scold Cat. We need ladybirds, I informed her, to deal with greenfly. (This Dr Doolittle habit of talking to birds, insects, animals and plants merely reinforces my neighbours' belief in my eccentricity.)

I finished the day by tidying up the front garden; the *Anemone Blanda* were beginning to uncurl blue flowers in their frilly leaf rosettes and the spears of daffodils were coming through well. What a glorious day!

* * * *

Spring continued to touch the earth tentatively for a few more days, then withdrew to let winter have a last thrust with icy claws and teeth in a stinging north-easterly wind. Straight from the frozen wastes of Siberia, it was the sort of wind too lazy to go round, so it went through all the layers of clothing you had to pile on. Several weeks of cold, sleet, wind, frost – almost every kind of weather that late winter still had up its sleeve – followed. The tender blossoms of the magnolia, fooled into emergence by the earlier sun, were now shrivelled and burnt by that bone-chilling wind.

But then, in the third week of March came another day – a Saturday this time – full of spring promise and sunshine with enough blue sky to make all the sailors in the Royal Navy a pair of bell-bottoms. (This saying was one of my mother's: 'If there's enough blue sky to make a sailor a pair of trousers, it will be a fine day.') I took advantage of it to spend hours in the vegetable patch.

Here I paid the price for having skimped the autumn digging. Add to my laziness a wet, relatively mild winter, and the result was a splendid crop of ground cover weeds: milfoil, hairy bitter-cress, pimpernel, groundsel, and the inevitable feral forget-me-nots. There

15

were also the perennial nasties turning up under the fork, and the ground was like black-and-sticky Christmas pudding. Tough going! But I was serenaded by the blackbirds and my ragged robin, and I watched early bees zooming home with their hind leg baskets packed full of bright gold crocus pollen.

Next door's cat came out again and rolled about in a warm patch on the path, exposing her tummy to the sun. She has an endearing habit of suddenly sitting up very straight on her hindlegs with her forepaws held delicately in front of her, tail straight out on the ground behind and ears pricked. In this position she looks like a cross between a kangaroo and a rabbit. She did this now, remaining thus for several minutes when her attention was caught by a rustly movement in the undergrowth on my wilderness neighbour's side of the fence.

One of his little dogs had come sniffing about and was minding his own doggy business, when he suddenly caught a whiff of Cat. Instant alarums and excursions! He went into more barking than would have been thought possible from such a small animal. Cat watched him rather disdainfully for a while, yawned and then settled into the leg-of-mutton position to wash her important parts. Dog was furious at this display of bravado and made several rushes at the fence, while increasing his volume of bark-and-growl-and-let-me-get-at-her noise by several hundred decibels. Cat ignored him, doing an extremely good imitation of Kipling's cat-who-walked-by-itself. My neighbour came out to haul Dog back to the house and give him a good talking to. I could hear Dog grumbling and muttering in frustration all the way up the path at the injustice of it all and at his Human Being's apparent inability to give him a fair hearing. I sympathised with him; Cat would not have been nearly so coolly nonchalant if there hadn't been the width of my garden and a good strong fence between them!

These early days in the garden, before the urgency of spring planting begins, are a definite bonus. They have a charm all their own, and a sense of there being time enough for all the work of the day to be completed between sun-up and sundown. Such days have to be treasured, before the busyness of spring sowing, summer working and autumn harvesting sets in, and you begin to wonder whether you really want to be a gardener – even of the amateur variety.

16

4

❀ ❀ ❀ ❀

OF BIRDS AND BEES, ETC
(with rather more of the former than the latter)

February 14th, in Europe (or at least in Germany) has a Valentine significance for the bird world; it is known as 'The Birds' Wedding Day'. Certainly, at about this time of year, there is a considerable flurry of feathered activity in and out of the ivy that grows thickly up the front cottage wall. From mid-February onwards I can hear many rustlings and flutterings, cheepings and squeakings, and the cheerful if completely tuneless twitter of sparrows.

(Sparrows are the squeakers and growlers of the bird world. All teachers who have ever had the task of forming a school choir will know the equivalent of these endearing, enthusiastic but tone-deaf birds. Later in the year, when the full-throated dawn chorus gets under way, the sparrows are relegated to the back row of the choir, so to speak, and instructed by The Choirmaster merely to open their beaks and not to squawk. Only when the chorus has finished its paean are they allowed to make a noise!)

Drawing back the curtains I can watch, over early morning tea, sparrow comings, goings and swoopings on bits of straw and twigs as the preparations for nest-building get under way. Other activities get under way too. This year there were considerable 'goings-on' from the end of January. Whether it was due to such mundane considerations as a particularly mild winter, or whether moral laxity had hit the bird world, there was certainly no such thing as waiting for The Wedding Day. Courtship seemed very short and sweet, to judge by the little cock-sparrows, who seemed (if you will pardon the expression) to get cockier by the minute; while numerous little hen-sparrows emerged from the ivy or the juniper bush looking decidedly ruffled about the feathers, and rather smug and pleased with themselves. By mid-March, it was plain that sparrow family considerations were coming along very nicely indeed, to judge by the forays on crumbs on the window-sill.

By mid-March too, the starlings were well into nest-building. Year after year, they have favoured numerous nest-places under the cottage eaves, and the path to the front door resembles a birds' building site. They really are the untidiest lot! Cowboy builders all, it's a wonder their eggs and babies don't fall through the floor of the mish-mash of twigs-and-things they call a nest. (Sometimes, sadly, they do. Sometimes, when sweeping up their building rubbish, I have found a tiny, pathetic featherless corpse among the twigs and leaves. I mutter imprecations against the careless parents, and give it a ceremonial burial, but there are always plenty of babies which survive to further the starling race). Their nest structures are such that not even a cuckoo will lay its eggs in a starling's nest; parasite it may be, but even a cuckoo has its pride.

Part of the problem is that the starlings seem quite unable to judge the suitability of nesting material; they try to push and weave long, unwieldy, unyielding pieces into the overall structure, which, when they won't stay put, they drop and scatter anywhere. And they make such a song-and-dance, such a squawk and chatter and argument about it all! Mr Starling comes flying in, trailing a stiff, brown iris leaf, three times as long as himself; Mrs Starling, scoldingly demanding to know how on earth he thinks they can make that fit into the half-finished structure, tugs it off him, pushing him off the gutter as she does so. He swoops back and grabs the other end, and as they both open their beaks to tell each other off, the leaf sails away on the March wind and ends up over the fence. Not a whit abashed, Mr and Mrs S. go on with their argument before flying off in different directions for more building stuff, most of which will end up littering my path.

In the Dawn of Time, when all created things were being brought into being, the birds, according to one legend, were asked by the Creator to choose the colours and patterns which would mark them and their descendants for ever. I can imagine the kerfuffle when it came to the turn of the prototype starlings. I can also imagine the Creator, having provided them with more than enough strut and cheek and mimicry, deciding in his wisdom to limit their colour choice to the more sober end of his palette. Just think what they would have been like with the scarlet and gold, blue and turquoise of the parakeets! Even so, they probably fell on the pots of black and grey and soft iridescent dark blue, shook them, knocked them over and stepped in them, fluttered and squabbled and threw spots and dabs and dashes at each other, so that they ended up speckled and freckled all over in an untidy hotch-potch. Thus they have remained for all time.

In spite of all their noise and chatter, you can't help liking them. They remain quite unrepentant over the mess they make of my garden path. To see them waddle and run about the garden, with their legs apart as though they had wet their knickers and neither noticed nor cared, simply makes you laugh. I also love their ability as mimics, which they share with a number of other bird species. Once, when working in another garden (not the one I have now) I was interrupted several times by the *brr brr* of the telephone. Each time, I dropped the spade and set off toward the house, only to find that the 'phone, exasperatingly, had stopped. Back to work, but a short while later, it sounded again. And again. And there in the willow tree was a cheeky starling, imitating beautifully the sound of a telephone, and nearly falling off his branch with glee whenever I was taken in by his trick.

Blue tits are pretty, tidy little birds, who seem happy to take advantage of our nesting boxes. A few years ago, when the biggest pine tree was still a tree, and hadn't been reduced through disease and felling to the mere stump it is today, a family of blue tits made use of the nest-box set high in the pine branches. On quiet warm days, the babies could be heard making small peep-peep-peep-peep noises, which, over the weeks, became louder and stronger. One Sunday, in late April, with the weather warm enough for us to sit in the garden for afternoon tea, we were immensely privileged to watch the babies' first outing from the nest.

Oh, my word, the excitement! Mum and Dad blue tit hopped and hovered about anxiously as the little ones made their first fluttery, unsteady flights. Only a few inches along the branch, or from one branch to the next one down, but how they squeaked and called:

'Look at me, Mummy!'

'Watch me, Daddy, I can fly!'

'I can do it too!'

'An' me! Whee-ee-eee!'

What a huge, bright, beautiful multi-coloured world they had emerged into. We did not dare to let ourselves think of wily cats, or hungry hawks, of the cold and rain, wind and drought that awaited these happy young hopefuls. Enough that it was spring, and the world was newborn and glorious, just for this one day.

5

❀ ❀ ❀ ❀

DAFFODILS ARE YELLOW – AREN'T THEY?

A surprisingly warm day in early April sent the children of the local primary school careering around their playground like kittens with the wind up their tails. The reception class in particular were in a surprisingly frisky mood, coming in from afternoon playtime on a gust of air that properly belonged to March, banging the door and scraping their little chairs with more noise than their teacher considered strictly necessary. 'Thank heaven it's nearly the end of term,' she thought, although that fact plus the sudden surge of spring sunshine were probably the main reasons for her usually docile tinies' extra bounciness.

'Settle down,' she commanded in her best no-nonsense tones. They were all going to make Easter cards to take home and she wanted to get the activity under way. Daffodils of thick paper were waiting to be coloured, cut out and stuck on to sky-blue cards; the crayon monitors were busy handing out the tins of coloured sticks while Miss B. explained the afternoon's task. 'And daffodils are yellow,' she announced firmly, mindful of a similar activity with last year's class which had resulted in a riot of multi-coloured *Narcissi*, the like of which had never been seen in the National Collection. Mind you, she had been short of yellow crayons last year.

She glared sternly at young Philip, her liveliest and naughtiest boy, who was brandishing a red crayon. Catching her eye he exchanged it for a blue one . . . She sighed and wondered fleetingly if he were colour blind, but dismissed the thought; his eyes were too full of mischief. She removed the offending crayon and pacified him with a bright orange one. The class grew quiet as unsteady lines of colour were whooshed across the flower shapes . . .

Of course, daffodils are yellow – aren't they? In the yellow band of the spectrum: from creamy white to primrose to buttermilk to buttercup to golden to all shades of orange. Everyone knows

21

daffodils are yellow. It was yellow flowers Shakespeare had in mind when he wrote of

> . . . daffodils,
> That come before the swallow dares and take
> The winds of March with beauty.

(Wish I'd written that.)

And what other colour would have caught Wordsworth's eye:

> Beside the lake, beneath the trees,
> Fluttering and dancing in the breeze?

Yellow daffodils dance everywhere: in town gardens, country gardens, pots, baskets, window-boxes and big park gardens; they cluster on roadside verges; wave to uncaring cars from roundabouts; curtsey to passing pedestrians from odd corners around the town; turn slightly sooty faces to the sky from city window-sills; flower bravely among the cans and paper bags on rubbish heaps. Even the most neglected garden will often have its yellow bits of cheerfulness among the weeds and long rank grasses. They might come in all sizes – from the tiny delicate miniatures, like 'Minnow' or 'Angels' Tears' to the large flamboyant favourite 'King Alfred'. But they come in all shades of yellow.

This contemplation of daffodil colour really began on a quiet evening one autumn, dozing by the fire with Cat on my knee and my favourite garden catalogue, perusing pages and pages devoted to *Narcissi* – all sizes and shapes of petals and trumpets, and shades of yellow . . . except that there, on page six, emblazoned 'NEW', was a picture of pink daffodils. Enraged, I flung the catalogue to the floor, and Cat leaped off my knee and took refuge behind the sofa. *Pink* daffodils! And a wishy-washy shade of pale pink at that!

'If I want pink flowers,' I shouted at Cat when he put a nose round the sofa to inquire if it was safe to come out, 'I wouldn't choose daffodils!'

The nose vanished again and I began to consider my totally illogical feeling of outrage. After all, most of us accept quite happily the man-made transformation of the humble and delicate primrose into more than five hundred varieties of *Primula*, which cover the whole range of colours from purple at one end of the spectrum to red at the other, and in all combinations. Tulips too come in all shades – even the famous black (about which I have some doubts). And what about roses? The hunt for the Blue Rose – which took years of careful research and resulted in a rather indeterminate mauvey-grey colour – did raise some objections from the more conservative among us.

While there are still some who like to know where they are as far as flower colour is concerned; A. A. Milne's tortoise being a prime example: he liked

> . . . to sleep in a bed
> Of delphiniums (blue)
> And geraniums (red),

most of us are happy with a little bit of experimentation. But only a little bit. Strange isn't it? An incredible amount of careful genetic crossings and mixings and breedings has gone on, ever since dear old Mendel played around with wrinkled and smooth-skinned peas. (Gregor Mendel, you will remember, was the Austrian monk-botanist who began experimenting with cross-fertilising peas and beans in his monastery garden. In so doing he discovered the laws of genetics.) This has produced not only a bewildering variety of leaf shape, plant height and flower colour (all of which we coo over at flower shows) but also resistance to nasty pests and diseases. Those who love gardens accept all this with delight, and rush to buy the very latest in technologically-assisted plants. Until, somehow, things appear to go a little bit too far, and we rebel. Well, some of us rebel.

'You can't gild the lily' my mother was fond of saying. But human beings have been gilding the lily – and blackening the tulips, blue-ing the roses and now pink-ing the daffodils – for centuries. It is perhaps all part of the urge to be creative, which is as much a Creator-given gift as anything else in humankind's make-up, and not only to be tolerated but definitely encouraged.

The other point of view, of course, is that it is 'people-interfering-with-Nature' and therefore to be deplored. It is interesting to speculate where we draw the line between being creative and being interfering. At some point (and in my case it was at the point of pink daffodils) some unease begins to creep in, and we start to worry about the ethical rightness of genetic engineering.

And whether human beings aren't (as always) getting a wee bit too big for their green wellies. A bit too presumptuous. Too exploitative. History has a way of coming up with disastrous consequences of our interference with nature; events which play havoc with our notions of being Lords and Ladies of Creation, and which scatter our pet theories to the four winds. If only we would learn the lessons of history, we might avoid future disasters and accept that at times we need to be neatly pruned down to size.

The afternoon sun was making the air somnolent in the reception class. Young Philip had finished his orange daffodil and he was embarking on colouring the leaves purple with horizontal blue stripes . . . Miss B. sighed again. That young man might go far as a twenty-first century Picasso. On the other hand – perhaps not.

6

❀ ❀ ❀ ❀

WATER IN THE GARDEN

Every garden, says my *Gardening Encyclopaedia*, should contain some water in the form of a pond, a bog-garden, a formal water garden or something.   There follow several pages of entrancing pictures taken by a professional photographer on a lovely summer's day, showing all kinds of beautiful watery idylls, from large still lakes reflecting sky and trees, to tumbling waterfalls, canals and Japanese bridges, and fountains of all shapes and sizes. I'm afraid I resisted this idea for many years, although I once took over a garden (well, actually a wild patch pretending to be a garden) which had a pond.   This 'Garden Feature' (in the estate agent's jargon) consisted of a shallow concrete-bottomed bowl, containing a few inches of rather slimy water, situated under a willow tree which shed into it thousands of leaves in autumn, and tens of thousands of fluffy seeds in early summer.   Trying to keep it ecologically balanced was a nightmare, and as I had a young family and little time for much garden work, I felt it had to go. Besides, we had a beautiful, natural, self-managing stream bordering the garden. What else did we need?

My present garden doesn't have a water-feature.   Both my neighbours, however, have water aplenty, so I can nod over the fence on one side to see and enjoy a whole range of pond-life, and listen to the tinkle and splash of a mini-fountain on the other.

My wilderness neighbour's pond is massive. A large oblong about the size of an average swimming pool; four feet deep at one end, tapering to a mere eight inches at the other, it is planted with six different kinds of water lilies; fringed with water forget-me-nots, irises, water marigolds and several other kinds of water and bog-loving plants, and home to innumerable snails, fish, frogs and water insects.   The upside of the insect inhabitants are the dragonflies; large and small, green, blue, bronze and gold.   The downside consists of various bloodsucking nasties, who like me far more than

I like them, and leave uncomfortable evidence of their partiality on my skin.

Working in the vegetable garden in the spring, I heard much noise and activity from the pond. This year spring fever gripped the frogs first, as they splashily obeyed the Creator's command to 'Go forth and multiply.' As there were only three females to about twelve males, there was a considerable amount of competition, indicated by much whooshing about and mad chasings up and down the pond. One large and obviously fecund female had a stairway of little males strung out behind her like a living train. The result of all this activity was enough multiplication of frogspawn to cover the whole pond surface, and my neighbour was kept busy building nursery tanks into which he shuttled off at least eighty percent of the production. Myriads of tiddly-wiggly tadpoles hatched out – and if only a small proportion of these finally made it into froggy adulthood the original parents should feel they merit a 'Well done!' from their Maker. The trouble is the new froglets will all return to their hatching pond to repeat the whole performance next year. My neighbour is already scratching his head over that one.

The fish were not far behind the frogs in this reproduction game, but they were rather shyer and less overt about the process. All that could be heard were deep plops as the males chased the not unwilling females around the pond, presumably successfully catching them among the lily leaves to judge by the increase in fishy population. Once again my neighbour was busy building nursery tanks, this time to take care of baby fishes – or exhausted motherfish. I presume he left the snails to their own devices. Perhaps a particularly wet winter and spring, which rendered the garden completely sodden, had provoked all this activity from the inhabitants of the water-world; perhaps they thought their time for taking over the earth had come.

What really impressed me was the joy and exuberance with which the birds, frogs and fish played the mating game. This is probably too anthropomorphic, but it seemed as though they were thoroughly enjoying themselves. I wonder why the human race has felt it so necessary to hedge the whole process about with taboos and rules, laws and regulations, forbidden fruits and unrealistic expectations. All of which lead to the sliding scale of prurience and prudery, priggishness and promiscuity. Now I am not advocating that humanity emulates the animal world (unless it be to follow the example of swans and stick insects, who mate for life); there has to be some restraint and consideration given to all aspects of human relationships. But shouldn't there be plenty of fun and joyousness about sex, which has nothing whatever to do with a nudge-nudge-wink-wink type of humour?

Water doesn't have to come in large areas. The best of Chinese gardens, although they frequently do have ponds and streams, also contain large-leaved plants which catch water on their broad tops, and gently dip and swing to let it run off in tiny rivulets. The Lady's mantle plant (*Alchemilla mollis*) does just that. After rain, it is wonderful to see how the drops run together into pearly globules across the surface of its round and deeply-veined leaves, and after a night mist, its frilly leaf-edges are fringed with miniature diamonds.

All too often, of course, there is too much blessed water. Last winter and into early spring, the rain it rainèd every day, so much so that the dips and hollows of the garden were well and truly waterlogged, and in the meadow garden the primroses were struggling against the rising flood. They poked pale, anxious little heads above the murky water, stretching their delicate stalks so that their flower faces resembled tiny water lilies, while below in the murky depths their rosettes of leaves turned brown and soggy, adding to the general gloopiness of the overall gloop. It was a relief when the heavenly taps were turned off somewhere about mid-May, and we could abandon thoughts that instead of gardening we should really be building another Ark.

By the end of July and into August we were beginning to feel that we had had enough of weeks of hot sun; the garden had completely forgotten its earlier waterlogged state and was crying out for rain, and the water companies were proclaiming a drought and sternly forbidding the use of hose-pipes . . . which provoked a delightful article in my favourite garden magazine on watering pots and cans. A quotation from 1706 on the forerunner of the modern watering-can describes it in almost poetic terms:

> Nothing is more useful in a Garden than a
> Watering Pot . . . it imitates the Rain falling
> from the Heavens; when being bended
> down it spouts forth water thro' a thousand
> holes that are in the Rose of it.

Apparently the shape and angle of the watering-can rose was the subject of careful early scientific investigation; it had to be so constructed that the shower of water should never fall with more than its own weight, and therefore never damage delicate shoots or disturb the soil around newly-planted seedlings.

But inevitably, the work of carrying water in cans over long distances has always been daunting (as no doubt our cousins in third-world countries can tell us from first-hand experience) so that even as early as medieval days, monks pioneered the art of conveying water to all parts of the garden in channels, conduits and pipes – which developed over time into hose-pipes – which of course are banned whenever we have a few days of drought!

P.S. Since writing this I have succumbed – and bought a small, self-contained jug-and-bowl fountain, which has room for gravel and water plants in its outer rim. Most attractive!

❀ ❀ ❀ ❀

7

ALL THINGS BRIGHT AND BEAUTIFUL
(including slugs and snails . . ?)

It's a favourite children's hymn isn't it?

> All things bright and beautiful,
> All creatures great and small,
> All things wise and wonderful,
> The Lord God made them all.

What's more, it has a pretty, if somewhat repetitive tune. But what about wasps?

My mother used to say: 'I see no reason for wasps,' thus perhaps unconsciously echoing Dylan Thomas's delightful comment on getting as a Christmas present a book 'that tells you everything you want to know about the wasp – except why'. Or as Schultz put it in a 'Peanuts' cartoon: 'Why didn't Noah swat both wasps while he had the chance?'

For some people the definitely-not-bright-and-beautiful creatures are spiders. Or ants. Or slugs and snails. So it is one of life's paradoxes that on Sundays we sing the Creator's praise for all things he has made: 'Yes, God is good, all nature says . . .' and on weekdays make forays into the garden shop for products with which to eradicate the creatures we do not happen to like: slug pellets, ant killers, insecticides, fly sprays, mole smokes . . .

We had a mole in our garden once. I had spent years – and I mean years – working to get a reasonable piece of grass which (daisies notwithstanding) I could call a lawn, only to find one morning that it had sprouted a row of unsightly brown earth humps. I am embarrassed to recall the words I uttered against the offending mole. We tried discouraging him with those supposedly effective smoke bombs but he ignored them and went on tunnelling and shovelling up more earthworks. The two cats (ours and our neighbour's) took a great interest in the line of humps, stationed themselves one at each end of it, and watched and waited. One or other of them had his patience rewarded because one morning we found the little black velvet gentleman stretched out stiff and cold, his large spade-like paws held up as if pleading for mercy. He looked so pathetic that I was filled with remorse. After all, what crime had he committed except to be in the wrong place at the wrong time?

In these days of ecological awareness, we can do quite a bit of unwanted-creature-eradicating without resorting to chemicals. A weak solution of washing-up liquid discourages greenfly, and beer, they say, can be a very useful slug eliminator. Put some in the bottom of a jamjar, plunge it in the earth near to the plants you want to protect from sluggy damage, and they (the slugs, not the plants) will fall in to an alcoholic end. Those who like beer may feel this is as good a way as any to go. So I scrounged round the house, but alas, the cupboard was bare of beer. We did have some orange-coloured-alcohol-smelling stuff that no-one had touched for years, so I used that. I caught *dozens* of slugs in my improvised slug-pubs . . . Later, my bemused husband informed me that I had spiked the jars with a most expensive liqueur. No wonder I caught so many; the pesky creatures probably came from miles around to die a bucolic death in my garden!

Coming back to the idea of all things being bright and beautiful: perhaps the hymn need not be taken to mean that all things are b-and-b, but that such b-and-b things as there are ('flower that opens, bird that sings, purple-headed mountain, river running by . . .') were made by the Lord God.

In which case, who made the others? Hmm . . . if we are not careful we shall find ourselves getting into a proper tangle, a real theological thicket that's worse than my blackberry bush, and that certainly does not seem to be on fire with inspiration. Let's go and sit under the old apple tree, which is in full blossom at the moment, with a large pot of tea. That's as good a place as any for the sort of serious thinking that goes back to First Things.

In the Beginning, God made all things, including light and seas, land and plants, fish and birds, insects and all land creatures. And us. (Whether this process took six days, or 60 billion years;

whether it was a once-for-all or a continuing-up-to-the-present-moment event need not concern us now. Nor can we get into a discussion about whether 'God' should be renamed 'chance'.) So far, so good. And it was good, as Genesis repeats like a solemn refrain. All things were splendid, bright, beautiful, wise, wonderful. So perhaps if we look carefully and with unclouded eyes at spiders, ants, slugs, black beetles or dragonfly nymphs we will see in them a kind of beauty, or at least an intricate pattern of light, dark, colour, shape, function . . . Wasps now: take away that ferocious sting and you have an insect of cheerfully banded colour with iridescent wings and a waist any girl would envy.

All right. I will concede that wasps have their own kind of beauty. And that spiders have a symmetry and patterning that is quite wonderful, as do ants. And the sheen and depth of blue-green colour on a so-called 'black' beetle's carapace is delightful. But slugs? Those brown or black splodges of slimy shapelessness with voracious mouths that can devour a patch of young seedlings in less time than it takes to write this? . . . The very name produces shudderings and squirmings and reachings for the slug jar . . . You want me to think of these as beautiful, Lord? Then you must give me different eyes to see with . . . I would rather have the wasp, sting and all.

But isn't that part of the problem? The wasp has to be taken as beautiful with the sting. You cannot take it away. Nor can you take away the tearing, scratching, biting, death-dealing teeth, claws and beaks of sleekly beautiful creatures such as cats (large and small), owls and other birds of prey. The amazing colour of the shy kingfisher may be a source of pure delight for us, but the hapless fish would probably not agree. A spider's web, all delicately hung with diamond drops on a dewy morning – is a death trap. We might think it a thing of beauty, but not so the poor insect thrashing about in its sticky threads, with the spider advancing to still its struggling victim with a swiftly paralysing bite. Ladybirds are the most delightful members of the large family of beetles, but if I were a greenfly, happily helping to demolish a rose, I would not be pleased to see this huge red creature coming down the stem to inform me of the error of my ways.

Under the surface of the observable, tiny grubs and insects, or even smaller bacteria and viruses, suck out the warm tissues and feed on the living brains of larger plants and creatures. And I have just been bitten by a gnat, who has injected an anticoagulant poison into my bloodstream, to judge by the itchy red lump on my arm. This puts me definitely on the side of the victimised: the worm in the bird's beak, the mouse in the owl's talons, the rabbit in the cat's jaws . . .

Was it all meant to be like this? 'Well, that's Nature, isn't it?' say my pragmatic friends, as though somehow that makes it all right, 'Things have to be kept in balance.' Yes, of course, but I don't have to like it, or agree with it. Why balance things out by death at the hands, or rather teeth, claws or slow lingering ingestation of and by other creatures? Is that what the Creator intended from the Beginning? And is that what was meant when he 'looked on the world he had made and saw it was very good'? If so, we need to think very hard about what is meant by 'good' and possibly to revise our notion of it.

But if not, did Someone Else put a spoke in the wheel? Someone Else who surreptitiously stirred things up, slipped in a few unsavoury changes and brought about death by pain, fear and slow decay. Both Isaiah (11:6-9) and St John the Divine (Revelation 21:4) look forward to the time or place when creatures will not hurt or harm each other, and death, pain and tears will cease to exist. It seems to suggest that they believed that the world as it is now (meaning the natural world and not counting what human beings have done to it) is not as it was originally meant to be.

Theologians don't like this idea (understandably) because it leaves the thicket still tangled up with too many unanswered questions which seem to lead to further questions, such as: Where did the Someone Else come from anyway? If we start taking away the bits we don't like from the natural world, then how will we ever know what had been intended in the first place? And how can we know what is 'good' unless there is a sort of 'bad' to compare it with?

All this takes us back to the Fruit of the Tree of Knowledge of Good and Evil, which the prototype Woman and Man should never have eaten in the first place, because if they hadn't then I wouldn't be sitting under this old apple tree asking unanswerable questions.

Perhaps I should have waited until autumn; Newton, after all, derived the notion of gravity out of sitting under his apple tree. All I seem to have achieved is a rather overworked brain and an empty teapot. So if you will excuse me I will go and spray the roses . . . they are covered with greenfly.

8

❀ ❀ ❀ ❀

FROM GARDEN TO WILDERNESS
TO GARDEN . . .

The lupins started this off on a train journey to Waterloo in early summer. I had been working on something that had seemed important as the train passed through Bracknell, Ascot, Sunningdale, Virginia Water, Egham, Staines . . . but just past Staines my attention was caught by large clumps of blue lupins alongside the track. Were they growing wild? Or were they garden-escapees, which had reproduced themselves all over a suitable spot? Certainly there were plenty of them, eye-catchingly pretty and nearly all purpley-blue, with the occasional white or yellow.

Later I looked them up in the wild-flower book and found there is a wild variety: *Lupinus nootkatensis* (poor thing!) which comes from North America; it can be found in shades of blue and purple and likes river shingle and moorland. In addition, the flower book mentioned the garden lupin: *Lupinus polyphyllus* (which makes it sound like something you use to fill cracks in a wall). This, having escaped the garden, spreads itself about in pink, white or yellow. There are also, apparently, several other kinds: *L. angustifolia*, *L. micranthus*, also known as the Bitter Blue Lupin and *L. albus*. These are all annuals and are: grown as crops, covered in brown hairs, and have white-flowers-tipped-with-blue respectively. What a mine of information the flower book is!

But the lupins alongside the railway raised the question: which came first? The Garden or the Wilderness? Chicken-or-egg? Serious-minded botanists will, perhaps, plump for the Wilderness-into-Garden theory. Many of our wild flowers are exceedingly pretty and have caught the imagination of humans-in-the-role-of-gardeners. Thus a particular plant might be carefully isolated, planted in a special place, kept fed and watered and free of all other more encroaching plants (which would then of course be labelled 'weeds') and given every kind of tender loving care to encourage it to grow larger and produce bigger, brighter, more beautifully coloured flowers.

Or else, following Mendelian principles, the seeds from certain flowers would be collected and nurtured; or different varieties carefully mixed and matched by brushing the stigma of one with pollen from another to produce new sizes, colours, shapes of flowers and leaves. Tracing the history of roses from the first simple wild briar to the amazing variety we have today, or daffodils, or almost any flower in our gardens, is a fascinating study.

In support of the Wilderness-to-Garden theory there are Plants that Travel. Many plants are carried purposefully by people into new places. Sailors and explorers brought back unbelievable tales of fantastic plants, so that doubting-Thomas botanists and plant collectors of previous (and present) centuries set out to see for themselves; to find new, exciting and rare wild plants in various odd spots of the world and bring samples and seeds back for their gardens and greenhouses. The lupins came from North America. Ah, but how did they get to North America? Were they indigenous, growing there in the wild open spaces naturally? Or were they taken there from the gardens of early European settlers and have therefore come home, many generations later?

I favour the Garden-to-Wilderness theory. Gardens go way back into history. The famous Hanging Gardens of Babylon are thought to have existed many thousands of years ago (how did they get the water up to them?) and the archaeology of the Middle East has turned up pots and urns filled with seeds, not all of them destined for food. Some of these thousands-year-old seeds, given water and soil, have germinated and grown, Rip-van-Winkles of the plant world, and proved their garden origins. So one can go back a long way to trace the theory that all our so-called wild flowers are really garden-escapees.

After all, they can and do manage to escape by themselves very effectively. Wind-blown seeds are no respecters of fences and walls and cheerfully sail over them into the wilderness beyond, where, although they may have to fight for space and don't have the gardener looking out for their welfare, may survive very successfully indeed. Nature books tell us of city dwelling plants, both in and out of the garden, that roll their seeds up in tiny mudballs and stick them to soles of shoes and car tyres, thus travelling miles from home before unrolling themselves into a new habitat. Others latch their seeds, velcro fashion, on to animal fur or people's clothing (and of course, velcro was invented from observation of the clever little curly hooks of burrs and goosegrass). If the shoes and coats in question happen to take to air or sea travel, well then, the seeds hitch a ride there too and end up anywhere on earth. If the climate and soil is right – and many of these travelling plants are extremely adaptable – then they settle down to a new life in a new land.

It is from the Middle East that we have the legend of the very First Garden, in the dawn of time, in the primeval history of the world. In the second and third chapters of Genesis we read that the Creator planted a Paradise Garden, from which flowed a river (all the best gardens having a water feature), which divided into four jewel-bearing tributaries: the Pishon, the Gihon, the Tigris and the Euphrates. In this King's Garden grew all kinds of plants, trees and flowers. Man and Woman were placed in this garden in order to look after it, meaning of course, that they had to work, even in Paradise. But, the story goes, they were tempted into wanting more knowledge than was deemed good for them; the kind of knowledge – like knowing in advance all the moves in a chess game – that only Divinity could handle. So they were turned out of the Garden into the wilderness, where life became a struggle against the elements, against thorns and brambles (horridness weeds?) and against the very earth which in the Garden had been so easily fertile. From sunrise to sunset and beyond they would have to work harder than ever before to produce enough food to keep themselves alive; flowers would be a luxury they could ill afford.

But I cannot help thinking that the Creator, although perhaps desperately disappointed in what should have been the best of his Creation, nonetheless provided a little bit of Paradise Garden on wilderness earth for his prodigal sons and daughters. Perhaps he allowed some flower seeds to escape by entangling themselves in Eve's hair and Adam's beard. Perhaps he filled the pockets of the garments he made for them with paradisal provender: fruit for their journey, to tide them over until the first crops came, and to give them apple-pips and plum-stones, and the seeds of soft fruits and the vine. Perhaps too, down in the corners of the pockets, he added the seeds of forget-me-nots – in the hope that they would remember him.

9

❀ ❀ ❀ ❀

OTHER PEOPLE'S GARDENS

A favourite pastime for many of us (confess it!) is to sneak a peek into other people's gardens. In many instances this does not have to be done at all surreptitiously: most front gardens are open to view, with very little to mark their boundary from the road or from their neighbours' plots. Others are a little more secretive, involving a peer through screening bushes or a tiptoe look over tall fences. A very few retain high walls, which always makes me long to climb up and look over because there must be something truly wonderful behind them. Lewis Carroll knew about the magic of this when he told of Alice's glimpse of a beautiful garden through a tiny and unreachable door.

But a short walk through the streets of a small town – Anytown will do – can be magic enough, and full of lessons to be learned about how to manage a garden, or not. In my own town the older terrace houses in a street in the town centre have no front spaces or gardens at all, but open straight on to the street. Nonetheless, a few people have managed to remove a paving stone from beside the front door and train a rambling rose or a clematis up and over the tiny porch. Several have window-boxes; some with magnificent swathes of trailing ivy, helichrysum, pelargoniums or petunias. One of the many public houses (our town should be in the Guinness Book of Records for its number of pubs) has some brilliant hanging baskets, but don't be fooled by them. They are filled with an incongruous mix of daffodils, geraniums, ivy and yellow and white chrysanthemums – all plastic. Still, they look colourful, don't need watering and last all year round.

The two best and most unusual features of this particular street are the rose on one side and the vine on the other. The former grows, scrambles and climbs all over the front of one of the oldest (seventeenth century) houses, and is covered with masses of pale pink flowers from June through to late September. The vine climbs and twines its way up and over the door of the Old Bakery (reminders of bread and wine), wriggles along the roof and hangs down over the porch of the cottage next door. The British summer seldom encourages much of a crop, but tiny clusters of pale green grapes can be seen in autumn, when the leaves turn a glorious red.

Further out into the suburbs, the houses and gardens are bigger. In many cases, especially where the houses go back 50 years or so, the front garden has been sacrificed to the great god Car. Sometimes this has been done sympathetically, and some interesting paved or gravelled spaces in various mixes of colour exist alongside what remains of the garden. More often than not, it is simply a square of tarmac. Alas, ecologists inform us that the increasing yardage of hard-stuff in towns and cities compounds the problem of water management. The 'gentle rain of heaven', instead of soaking into the earth to water root and engender shoot, now has considerably less earth to soak. Instead, a high percentage of it runs off the roads and hard-standings straight into the drains and down into the sewage system, taking with it the bitsam and bobsam of urban life: grit and grime; dog-ends and matchsticks; engine oil and pesticides; crumbs and crisp packets. A sudden heavy shower, thunderstorm or merely two or three days of steady drizzle after a spell of dry weather, instead of relieving the dry ground and raising reservoir levels, simply floods the drains, blocks the pipes and backs up the amount of sewage in the pipes below the streets, which then overflow – with mucky consequences!

Square seems to be the favourite shape for most front gardens: a square of grass, with maybe a tree of some kind somewhere in the middle, with a square of border like the edge of a hanky all round. But here and there lively imaginations have been at work; meandering paths, stones set into the grass, or borders of different shapes and sizes break up the inevitable square plot. Trees and bushes of different heights also add interest. But several gardens really stand out from the ordinary, and would earn prizes for ingenuity.

Let's present the Garden Oscar awards – in the shape of a Gnome perhaps? Now this one would definitely earn a prize; it's an absolute riot of colour all year round. It's small, and has no grass; an oval narrow paved path runs round the inside of the general square shape, so that the outside borders, and the small one with the oval can be easily reached and worked. It is filled with all kinds of everything in every season: against a backdrop of here-and-there small conifers are colourful heathers, pansies and primulas in winter; all the bulbs there are in spring, and a mass of summer flowering annuals. But in autumn it comes into its own with dahlias, multifarious chrysanthemums, nerines, colchicums, cosmea (aka Japanese Anemones) all blazing with bright pink, scarlet, crimson, gold, cream, yellow, white . . .

Another meritorious garden has obviously been designed along Chinese lines. Again, there is no grass, but raised beds edged with vertical wooden posts create a curvy central space. The beds contain heathers, mini-conifers and small Alpine rockery plants set in gravel and woodchips of different colours. The central space is filled with large gravel raked into lines and patterns, with a cluster of white, brown and grey rocks set together slightly off centre. Various spiky grasses grow about the stones, and a smiling but extremely pot-bellied Buddha surveys his small domain and the passers-by with benign indifference. I wonder where they would put the Gnome?

This next garden would have no problem finding space for its Gnome Award – one would be quite at home sitting among an arrangement of a dozen of its brothers along the top of the porch from which hang huge flowering baskets. The garden has spilt out of its square confines, edged with council-provided chainlink fencing. It has scrambled round and up and over and through the fence, spilling on to the pavement with the purple-blue bells and stars of *Campanula arvatica* or *glomerata*; it has encroached on to the path and climbed the house walls in baskets and pots of all shapes and sizes, and boxes swing under every window with leafy exuberance. As well as all this florabundance, it is set about with yet more gnomes of various occupations. These red-and-green cloned individuals have been put around the garden to work with spades and hoes, wheel-barrows and trowels, and fishing rods hung over a puddle of a pond. In addition there are cats and snails (rather disconcertingly these are the same size); a stone heron eyeing the cheerful fishing gnomes with disfavour; a windmill and a large shoe, from which the Old Woman and all her offspring have disappeared – to find accommodation elsewhere perhaps?

Two doors down another Gnome Oscar might be awarded to a precise, geometrically organised miracle of garden neatness. The oblong of fine grass is so smooth, even, weed-free, closely-shaved-and-short-back-and-sides-cut (not a daisy in sight) as to resemble a billiard table. Its edges are precision-trimmed, even along the rosy-hued tiled path, where it is scalloped to form small hexagonal indentations. Each of these contains a single deep pink *Begonia Rex*, identical in size and shape. Under the window are six paving slabs, alternating pink and green in colour and set diamond-wise to each other. Three tubs, equidistantly spaced, contain geraniums of the exact shade of pink as the begonias. The whole is divided from the street by a low box hedge, evenly cut with perfectly square edges. This controlled study in green and pink is rescued from boredom by one flaw – accidental or intended, it's impossible to tell which. The third begonia from the front door – is white.

At the other end of the scale there are so-called gardens that make your fingers itch to get at them. In this patch we have a goodly crop of thistles; in that one the grass and horridness weeds have grown thigh-high. This one is a graveyard for old bikes and rusting hulks of cars. But some of these spaces – which cannot be called gardens – have their charm and uses: one in particular is an adventure playground for the children. Here, using logs and sticks, old blankets, clothes-lines, spades and stones, their imaginations have carved out dens and caves, dungeons and dragons, prairies and mountains. Here the children are rulers of their universe and masters all of their own destinies.

Perhaps the saddest sight is of a once cared-for garden run to neglect, or of roses that continue to flower bravely in spite of straggly, tangly unpruned growth. Paul, in his letter to the Colossians, advises new Christians to 'mortify their members', by which I think he means they should ruthlessly prune out of themselves all their old ways of behaviour 'on which divine retribution falls'. Rather like pruning a rosebush: first we need to cut out the dead wood – all those hang-ups, habits, resentments and chips-on-the-shoulders we have kept from our early days; then we must prune out the cross-tangly shoots – the bits of bad behaviour that interfere with our relationships; cut away the suckers – fruitless aspects of which the General Confession says, 'we have done those things we ought not to have done . . .' Finally we have to prune down the good shoots to the second leaf-bud to encourage healthy growth.

There is a sorry-looking rosebush around the corner from my cottage, which looks as though it has never been pruned. One of these days I shall creep out at dead of night with a torch in one hand and secateurs in the other and give it a good going over. I wonder if the owners would notice?

10

❀ ❀ ❀ ❀

PHILOSOPHY OVER THE GARDEN FENCE

We have a division of labour in our garden: my husband does the hardware (paths: removal, renovation and laying of; patio and walls: building of). I do the software, which, of course, is everything else. However, in the early days when we were laying the foundations, so to speak, I was roped in to help with remaking the path alongside the vegetable plot. We didn't have access to a concrete mixer at the time, so it was the back-breaking mixing-up-by-hand work for the male of the species and the spreading, smoothing and scraping for me. Our neighbour came down his garden to ask how we were getting on. 'I know people like that there concrete,' he observed, 'all soft and manageable at first, then they set hard in their ideas and you can't shift 'em for love or money.'

Well, when you are expecting something about the weather, or some other kind of mundane remark with which we usually make social contact, a comment like that rather takes your breath away. But as we were to find out, our neighbour had, and continues to have, a tendency to surprise us. He is not particularly remarkable in appearance – slim and neat, with a round face that often carries a look of some surprise, and with a tiny hand-rolled cigarette in the mouth of it. He worked for an engineering firm, having left school at fourteen, but he is also an artist of some considerable but totally natural talent across a whole range of art forms: music, writing and painting.

Most of his paintings reflect his great love of Nature: trees, landscapes and sometimes reproductions of famous paintings. Here, his practical skills come in useful, for he spends time inventing small tools – tiny rollers with different textured ends, scrapers of various shapes and spiky brushes – and with these he achieves a number of interesting effects. He has also made excursions into more modern 'representative art'. He called me into his shed-cum-studio once to show me a small piece of wood on to which he had stuck various bits of tools, nails, jam-pot lids, fabric, wool, twigs, leaves . . . He explained animatedly that it represented the progression – or rather regression – from the fluid, swirling shapes of Nature to the square, straight, boxy artifacts of human invention.

Now I have often thought that this 'modern' art stuff is just so much chicanery; as in the story of the Emperor's New Clothes, we are beguiled into thinking that there is much more to it than we can see, and if we can't see what there is then we are fools . . . But when my neighbour explained with so much delight and enthusiasm what he was trying to represent I could begin to see it – I think. Unless, of course, he was fooling both of us.

On another occasion he gave us something he had written, which was quite delightful: it raced breathlessly through its story-line without stopping for commas and not too many full stops either rather like Mark's Gospel it went on and on in a hurry with the ideas coming thick and fast because it had so much it wanted to say and apparently not a lot of time in which to say it and therefore it all had an air of most tremendous fun and excitement about it!

On yet another occasion, he played us some of his vocal jazz – recorded on a mini-cassette (which had to take the place of musical stave and notation, such being outside his experience). The jazz came straight from his head and heart. Move over the Swingle Singers! This was good stuff!

But it is Nature (always with a capital N) that holds him in such thrall. He is forever amazed by it: its burgeoning, flowering and fruiting, its colours, shapes and fluidity. He is constantly delighted with the way it can and should appeal to all our senses, and in contrast constantly bewailing the fact that only in man-made things do you get straight lines and square shapes: 'There are no squares or straight lines in Nature,' he says. When he was renovating his shed-studio, which needed new windows, I suggested he put in round or oval ones. He was thrilled with this idea, but alas, it was impractical and they remained square. So he draped the edges with material to soften them up a bit.

On warm summer evenings and at weekends, he sits in his garden, sometimes reading books on philosophy (honestly!) and sometimes just looking. 'Lots of colour everywhere,' he says, 'and if you just take one colour – say green – there's lots of greens, more than in my paintbox; more shades of green than I can mix up with all the blues and yellows. Some people say, "Oh well, they're just leaves" – but just look at all the different shapes and greens, and some are shiny and some've got deep lines on 'em . . .'

Then he would shut his eyes for a bit.

'You asleep?'

'No, jus' listening. There's a noise at all levels: up in the trees where the birds are, and down here with the bees buzzin' and the fountains, and the cat scratching, and farther away someone with a mower. I bet if our ears were sharp enough we could hear the worms wigglin' and the snails munchin' . . .'

'I hope they're not munchin' my new plants,' said his wife. (She had just put in a row of new primulas, the large Belladonna daisies, and various *Dianthus* plants, and was convinced that the slugs and snails for miles around were telling each other about the new restaurant opened at number 35. I had agreed to lend her my slug-pubs to make it a licensed establishment.)

'And there's somethin' for our noses,' he went on, 'smell that honeysuckle, and that white flower – what is it?'

'*Philadelphus*, 'Mock Orange',' I said, from over the fence. 'It's beautiful.'

'So's the smell of dinner cooking, and I suppose in no time you'll be askin' for it,' and his wife went off to the house.

'That's eyes and ears and noses accounted for,' I said, 'but what about touch?'

'Warm sun and little breezes making goose-pimples on your skin.'

'And taste?'

'Ah! That's my beer!' said my neighbour, suddenly coming down to earth and taking a long swig. 'But that came from Nature as well, o'course!'

Where did he get his childlike wonder, his depth of reverence for the glory of the natural world, his curiosity, his creativity, his sense of the numinous? When the young blue tits were beginning to make their little peep-peep-peep noises in the nesting box, he came and stood with his ear to the trunk of the old pine tree and listened with a look of absolute wonder and delight on his face.

'All this Nature going on right under our eyes-and-ears-and-noses,' he said, and then sadly: 'So many don't notice it, you know, don't even know it's there!'

He who has ears to hear, let him hear.

His family remain amused but occasionally exasperated. His wife, who runs the house, garden, family and part-time job with superb efficiency, and who is also a wonderful plants-woman has been heard to comment: 'Just look at that! He's so busy gawpin' around that he don't notice where he puts his big feet, especially in the garden.' (This when finding a rather squashed prize plant.) But on the whole they view his eccentricities with tolerance.

As Paul reminds us, we all have different gifts. And as Jesus taught us in the parable of the talents, it is very much up to us what we do with them. The gift of wonder should be nurtured as much as any other, for by this we remain childlike – and of such is the kingdom of heaven. It is good, and sometimes necessary, to wallow in the mud (especially at the time of the spring and autumn digging), but it is also important that, like my neighbour, we look up now and then and marvel at the leaves, the flowers, the birds and the stars.

11

✿ ✿ ✿ ✿

HARVESTING FRUIT

My present garden is long and narrow – approximately 150 by 15 feet. Both house and garden are old; the house was built at the turn of the century, along with half-a-dozen others as farm workers' cottages. The original house would have been a simple two-up-two-down with a washroom and an outside earth closet; the garden would have housed the family pig or chickens (or both) at the long end. The contents of the earth closet would probably have been spread about to add to the present fertility of the soil, and the end of the garden, where the pig and chickens used to be, and which is now the fruit-and-vegetable plot, has the richest, darkest, stickiest soil of all. Obvious really.

So our currant bushes are extremely productive. We have six blackcurrant, three redcurrant (one was a whitecurrant, but deciding early in its career that it was outnumbered, it reverted to red), three gooseberry and a goosecurrant. Yes, honestly. This last was a present from Nina, one of my gardener friends, but it hasn't produced much in the way of fruit. I think it feels a bit overwhelmed and is not very happy about its mixed parentage. Perhaps all the other fruit bushes (with the possible exception of the once-whitecurrant) are rather snooty about their own pedigrees, but whatever the reason, the goosecurrant produces a mere handful of interesting fruits, rather like smooth black gooseberries, to the others' pounds and pounds of berries.

Talking of mixed-up plants, we also have a damson tree that decided it wanted to be a plum, and a very elderly apple tree that produces two very different types of apples: one large, sweet, juicy reddish-gold with a distinct resemblance to a Cox's orange pippin, which does not break down in cooking; the other smaller, green and very sharp-tasting, which cooks into a beautiful fluffy mush. The damson-plum tree, which we planted ourselves, took a long time to get going (perhaps because it could not make up its mind what sort of tree it was) but produced a pretty show of blossom each year. My friend Mary B. warned me not to take much notice of this, however; plum trees tell fibs, she said, especially if they ought to be damsons. She was right: for the first five years we had about two or three indeterminate little black fruits, bigger than damsons but smaller than plums; in year six we had at least a dozen slightly larger fruits, but this year it fulfilled its early spring blossom promise and yielded twenty pounds of small but proper plums, resembling Purple Pershores and tasting absolutely delicious.

By early-to-mid-June the redcurrant bushes are swinging with long strings of beautiful fruit: translucent red berries which rival the most costly rubies for bright shininess. Who needs precious stones? Especially when you can eat these in puddings, pies, jams and jellies. I gather at least twenty pounds of fruit from each bush, and that is without covering them with nets or a fruit cage. The birds are allowed their share; indeed I need them to help with the harvest, or there would be more than I could cope with.

Blackcurrants come a bit later, and you have to wait and watch carefully so as not to pick them too soon. Each currant has to be a true, shiny black, with no suggestion of redness about it, and it must tumble softly off the stalk into the basket. My mother taught me to make the best blackcurrant jam in the world, and part of her secret (I'm not going to reveal it all!) is to ensure that the blackcurrants are really ripe. Slightly unready ones end up as 'boot-button jam': small hard currants – resembling the tiny black buttons on Victorian ladies' high boots – floating in a dark red liquid.

The gooseberries are also prolific, although picking these can seriously damage your fingers. I wonder why babies are said to be found under gooseberry bushes? Of all the uncomfortable places to get oneself born, even in legend. Perhaps it was felt to be prophetic for the poor little mites; if they could survive a gooseberry bush for the first experience of the world then they would learn to cope early with the 'slings and arrows of outrageous fortune' that life would throw at them. However, my babies came in the usual fashion, and the only things to be found under my gooseberry bushes are the over-ripe berries which eluded the picking, and which then set about growing into new plants . . .

. . . Which brings me to contemplate bountiful Nature, scattering her treasures with profligate hand, as the poets are fond of telling us. Taking a break from redcurrant picking one day and sitting under the bushes with a cup of coffee, I opened up a single redcurrant and began to work out mathematically just how profligate nature was with respect to my laden plants. My one moderately-sized redcurrant contained 17 seeds; there were 29 currants to the ounce (I weighed and counted them later), and therefore 493 seeds to every ounce of berries. So in every pound of fruit there would be approximately 7,888 seeds and every currant bush – which gives about 20 pounds of fruit – produces over 157,760 seeds. And each one of those little pips, which so annoyingly get between your teeth and have to be flossed out and spat down the sink, could grow into a new currant bush. Each seed, minute as it is, contains all the necessary genetic blueprint information for roots and woody stem, branches and leaves, small flowers and shiny red berries. I shall spit them out with great respect in future.

In my garden I have three bushes, so multiplying up yet again, potentially it could contain 473,280 redcurrant bushes. In the space of a few years each of these would start to produce its own crop of currants, each currant containing 17 seeds . . .

I hastily finished my coffee and set about picking the berries which would end up as pudding, or jam. But my mind, like the sorcerer's apprentice, went on doing calculations. What about the days when, assuming the seeds survived the cooking process, they would (excuse me) pass through the human digestive system and end up in the earth closet, the contents of which – as mentioned earlier – were spread about the garden? It could become a wilderness of currant bushes. There would be nothing but currant bushes as far as the eye could see. The whole earth would be one large garden of redcurrant bushes endlessly spreading themselves, and I haven't started counting the blackcurrants, gooseberries, strawberries, raspberries, apple-pips, plum-stones!

Except, of course, that the Gardener in his wisdom and generosity has made allowances for various contingencies. He may well be telling us that such profligate generosity is a Divine quality which we would do well to emulate. Sharing resources is what harvest is all about after all. Harvest prayers remind us that nature is a prodigal and open-handed giver, and in Psalm 104: 28 it says:

'When you open your hand, they
eat their fill of good things.'

Why, then, are so many still hungry?

12

❀ ❀ ❀ ❀

GARDENS OF MEMORY

In 1947, aged six, I was picked up from an East London tenement and set down on the edge of a small Essex town – where I instantly took root and thrived. It was the slightly up-market end of that Cockney holiday paradise: Southend-on-Sea, famous for its longest pier (necessitated by miles of malodorous worm-wriggling mudflats), saucy postcards and gaudy hats, candy floss and the famous Southend Illuminations, which rivalled those of Blackpool for ingenuity. We lived at the Leigh-on-Sea end of what later became one large industrialised conurbation, but which in the 1940s and '50s still contained many pockets, corners and spaces where no houses stood, no roads ran and no high-rise industrial buildings broke the view of wide, cloud-piled Essex skies.

The bungalow where my adoptive parents lived had been built in 1921. They bought it – on a mortgage of course – for the huge sum of £350. It stood in a row of similar little bungalows with a wide field bordering its spacious garden, and one of the afore-mentioned spaces to the front of it. This hummocky, bumpy, weed-strewn space was a natural adventure playground for children by day and a hunting ground for cats by night. Miniature paths ran round rocks and through jungles – all huge in a child's small world. It was the perfect place to play cops'n'robbers, cowboys'n'indians, hide'n'seek, treasure hunts, or simply 'he'. Mothers could keep an eye on their offspring from the houses on the other side of the lane. Although officially called a 'Drive', to try and drive anything down its unmetalled, pitted and pockmarked surface necessitated a speed of no more than 15mph. Not that there was much traffic anyway; petrol was – if not still on the ration – at 1/9 (7p) a gallon way beyond people's means for everyday consumption. Deliveries such as milk, coal and vegetables came by horse and cart. My mother would sometimes set me to watch for the droppings from the milkman's horse; to such excellent gardeners as my parents, horse manure was much prized. A goodly dollop in the vicinity of our house was a lucky day, and would send mother out with a shovel and pail – and a few furtive looks in case the neighbours were watching. Not that they would have minded, but she always ensured she had her apron on for this activity, not so much to protect her dress, but as a kind of disguise. 'People don't see me in the street in an apron,' she would say. Fifty years later, I am still puzzling over her logic.

If you went up the Drive from our house, turned left on to the main road and crossed over, you would come to Belfairs. This was (to a small six year old) a vast area of woodland, which also contained two golf courses – a full eighteen-hole and a miniature nine-hole course. This latter was not a putting green, nor that later invention called crazy golf, but a proper scaled down version of the real thing with bunkers and rough surrounds. The wooded part of Belfairs was full of wildlife: badgers, squirrels, foxes, birds and butterflies. Here I learnt my first botany lessons from my knowledgeable father in summer, and helped him gather twigs and dead wood for our stove in frosty winter. The winter of 1946-7 was particularly long and bitter, and coal was expensive. My parents could afford to fill the little coal shed only once a year, and that had to last the whole season, so forays into the wood to gather sticks assisted our economy and also helped to keep the woodland floor clear.

As the days lengthened and grew warmer, the doors to the garden were flung open, and remained open. If the waste ground to the front was our wilderness, rough-hewn with rocks and rank with weeds, then the garden was my Eden, my Paradise. Generous by adult standards, it was huge to a child, and had been created from a wasteland by my father, whose epitaph reads: 'He inherited a wilderness and bequeathed a garden.' Standing with your back to the house, on the left were three small sheds – for wood, coal and garden tools. A magnificent patch of *Oxalis Novalis* grew alongside these, and I loved to note whether its bright flowers were closed into their long bell-shape on dull days, or opened into pink stars when the sun shone. Behind the sheds, and running the length of the garden was the fruit and vegetable patch. Currant bushes, rhubarb, root vegetables, salad greens, tomatoes or potatoes abounded here. This part of the garden was, after all, the main recipient of the horse dollops.

At the bottom of the garden a latticed screen sectioned off the compost heap. One of father's least favourite jobs was turning this over twice a year and forking out the soft and crumbly bottom-of-the-heap muck, to spread over the beds before the spring and autumn planting.

A tall fence marked off the back boundary, with a ditch beyond giving on to the playing field. You could tell the seasons according to the sounds emanating from here: thumps, roars and whistles denoted football in winter; a smack, crack and slow handclap meant cricket in summer.

The rest of the garden was laid out with lawn and flower beds, and we had three fruit trees: a Bramley apple and two plums – Purple Pershore and Victoria. (My mother's plum jam was very nearly as good as her blackcurrant.) A hazelnut tree stood against the right boundary fence, and a thornless blackberry clambered over the garage wall. A huge oak grew just outside the bottom right corner, scattering leaves and acorns a-plenty but also providing welcome shade across that quarter of the garden. The grass under the tree was left rough to contain daffodils, primroses and bluebells.

That was the first garden I knew and I have carried its memories through into all the other gardens I have grown. Memories of helping with the bulb planting in early winter, and picking a bunch of daffodils for the breakfast table in spring; in summer the high flowering of the herbaceous border, picking currants and smelling their hot conversion into wonderful jam, gathering lettuce and tomatoes, playing all kinds of make-believe games in the garden, with leaves, rose petals and acorn cups furnishing an imaginary dolls-house, or simply sitting in the shade, reading adventure books and fairy stories. In autumn there was the plum and apple harvest, and helping to store the latter in rows on newspaper in the loft, making sure each one did not touch its neighbour, so that if one went rotten, it did not set off the others. (There has to be a lesson in that somewhere.) Washing winter cabbages with the water running into pearly drops on the soft green, and gathering ripe hazelnuts ready for Christmas. My father pruning the apple tree, and saving the largest branches for burning, also at Christmas, for there is nothing quite like the smell of burning apple wood. What more could be asked of any childhood?

That garden was not the only one I remember and associate with my father. Later, when I was grown up and had children of my own, he moved, after my mother's death, to another small cottage with a long garden, which, on the removal day (which was in midsummer and therefore in the school holidays) was more like a hay meadow than anything else. My children plunged into the high grass with whoops of delight, and promptly disappeared! Four waving lines marked their progress and they returned – blissfully filthy – when all the work of moving in was done. A few weeks later, the grass had been scythed to a manageable length; flower beds and a vegetable plot had been marked out, a garden shed-cum-playhouse organised, a climbing-frame for the children put up, and a garden began to take shape out of the wilderness.

My father's last garden was a small town one, thick with shade, heavily weedy. He shook his head over this; after all he was getting on in years and I think it presented rather more of a challenge than he would have liked. But nothing daunted, he set to work and created a peaceful haven of soft colour, with a wondrous bog garden across one damp corner.

I remember too the gardens belonging to my green-fingered family. Uncle Harry's was a tree-shaded bower with little herring-bone-patterned red-brick paths that meandered around going nowhere in particular, looking-glass-world fashion. Aunt Rose's large and rambling garden had a marvellous apple tree (which I was allowed to climb) and a grassed-over hump of an air-raid shelter, starred with primroses and small pink daisies. It also had a beautifully tended cemetery plot for deceased household pets. Aunt Dolly's acres, which she managed herself up to and beyond her ninetieth birthday, were full of little snippets and seeds of things she had begged or been given from friends and neighbours (and occasionally from places like Kew when no-one was looking) that had grown and flourished under her tutelage into a magnificently full garden.

The balcony and window-boxes of Aunt Gertrude's flat in Wimbledon held an incredible mix of all kinds of everything, including lettuces, tomatoes and strawberries. I thought this flat absolutely the last word in elegance; it had lofty rooms, thick embossed wallpaper and delicate chandeliers. Aunt G. herself was elegant, at least in her working life as a fashion buyer for Derry and

Toms (which was famous for its roof garden – one of the wonders of pre-war London). But when she was pottering about on her balcony she didn't worry about elegance. An old headscarf over the coiffed hair, hands plunging deep into the potting compost; who cared about dirt under the fingernails? What was important were the plants and the growing. Thus I had my first lessons in container gardening.

But the most important lesson imparted by my relations, (implied rather than taught) was that in Life as in Gardens you should perhaps try and leave it just that little bit better than when you found it. (My mother applied this rule even to public toilets.) Or quite a lot better. Certainly more colourful, more beautiful, more useful, more organised. 'He inherited a wilderness and bequeathed a garden.'

Nice epitaph – I think I'd like it for mine.

13

❀ ❀ ❀ ❀

ALL AMONG THE HERBS

The herb garden (or patch if you feel the bit where the herbs grow isn't large enough to be dignified with the name 'garden') is a wonderful place to be in late summer or early autumn. Weeding, pruning and gathering herbs preparatory to drying them for winter use and storage is deliciously aromatic, and at the end of an hour or so spent all among the herbs in the autumn sun you smell rather better than, say, when turning the compost heap or spreading manure.

Most of us grow a number of herbs for cooking: mint and parsley, sage and thyme, chives and rosemary, maybe even lovage and fennel, tansy and rue. We are also aware of their health and healing properties, and may be willing to experiment with tisanes and syrups, although you have to know what you are doing with what if you don't want to end up with a bad attack of collywobbles.

Many herbs are still used in twentieth-century medicines, perhaps rather more circumspectly than in previous centuries, when herbalists relied on lore, legend and the wondrous Doctrine of Signatures to guide their diagnoses and prescriptions. This doctrine stated that the Creator had provided a sign on every plant by which people might know what disorder it would cure. Thus the purple of irises meant they could be used to cure bruises; spotty cowslip flowers were obviously intended for all spotty complaints. Lungwort (*Pulmonaria officinalis*) has lung-shaped leaves, hence both its name and the idea that it was good for wheezes and sneezes. Unfortunately, there was plenty of room for error, and many trials were needed to decide which plant could be used for what. I suspect innocent faith also came into the process of healing somewhere – it still does.

There are many beautiful and knowledgeable books on herbs (I have some on my shelves) and most have the seriously estimable purpose of being practical guides in the growing and using of herbs for culinary, medicinal, cosmetic or aromatic purposes. From various sources I have collected some of the old legends and stories that surround many of the plants that have been growing in someone's garden somewhere for thousands of years. So, with acknowledgement to all herbals from Anglo-Saxon times to the nineteenth century, here is my own (limited) alphabet of herb-lore. (Inevitably in a personalised list of this kind there will be many omissions, so if your favourite herb isn't included, many apologies.)

A is of course for APPLE – some trees are considered 'herbal' in the sense of having flowers or fruit of healing – and the apple tree is a symbol of fruitfulness. Strange that the apple is equated with the Forbidden Fruit, and the symbol of sexual temptation. Neither idea has any grounding in the book of Genesis. In medieval days it was thought that apples could cure warts and rheumatism – as a poultice of rotten apples slapped on to the affected parts.

B is for BAY, and has a biblical reference: 'I have seen the wicked flourish like the green bay-tree' (Psalm 37:35, although some versions have 'cedar of Lebanon' and others 'green tree in his native soil'). The reference seems to suggest not that the Bay is wicked but that it flourishes. Which it does – well, mine does – in a large pot that gets shunted around the garden for various reasons and which has been frozen, heated, soaked or dried out according to the caprices of the British weather, but which continues to grow ever green, and to produce pretty creamy flowers in late spring. The Greeks dedicated Bay to the god of healing, Aesculapius, and sixteenth-century herbalists extolled its virtues against devilry and witchcraft, thunder and lightning, snakebite and 'the eville of all kings' (whatever that was). Though how they read all that from the Doctrine of Signatures I cannot imagine. B is also for BORAGE, with its country name of Bee-bread, because bees love it. Another name for it is Cool Tankard; its leaves put into a claret or fruit cup have the power to expel sorrow – or so they say.

Bees also adore *Cotoneaster* – digressing from herbs for a moment. I have watched all kinds of bees go bumbling up and down my *Cotoneaster* bush, poking and pushing into the tiny pinky-white flowers almost before they have had a chance to unfurl their little petals. It has nothing to offer our noses, but the bees won't leave it alone from morning to night, until they finally reel drunkenly away into the evening, probably to be scolded by the Queen when they get back to the hive for staying out so late.

The seeds of DILL and FENNEL are well-known for enhancing the flavour of fish and cucumber, but were also known in Puritan America as 'meetin' seeds'. Concentration on the long Sunday services, to which everyone was expected to go fasting, could be helped by nibbling on these tiny seeds; apparently they helped to prevent the grumbles of empty tummies. F is also for FOXGLOVE (*Digitalis purpurea*), famous for its use as a source of the drug used for heart disorders (not to be used without medical supervision, as it is poisonous). Its various country names are as pretty as the plant itself: Goblin Thimbles, Witches' Thimbles, Fairyweed, Gloves of Our Lady and Snoxums.

GARLIC is powerful – and powerfully pongy – with a long history going back to Egyptian times. The Romans gave it to their slaves and soldiers to promote strength and courage. Imagine the whole Roman army exhaling garlic as they advanced shouting and yelling – no wonder they were invincible; their enemies were probably overcome by the fumes. Seventeenth-century herbalists thought that garlic was a panacea for all ills, and indeed it has antiseptic and disinfectant properties: in World War I it was used in powdered form in open wounds. But it can be invasive in some parts of the country – spreading into the lawn to make mowing an intensely olefactory and eye-wateringly painful experience. I love this early 'Receipt for the Cure of Measles':

> Take a piece of homespun linen and tare (sic) into nine pieces, sprede each with powdered garlic from different bulbs. Wrap around the child and nurse for nine days. Bury the nine pieces of linen in the garden and every measle will fall from the child and follow the garlic.

(Measles usually clears up in about nine days anyway!)

We will ignore HEMLOCK and HENBANE; these are witches' herbs, highly poisonous and used to conjure up spirits and give powers of clairvoyance (although some medieval herb-doctors advocated bathing the feet in henbane to cure insomnia). HORSERADISH is one of the 'bitter herbs' of the Jewish feast of the

Passover, and was used medicinally as a throat gargle. But its roots, like those of mare's tails, grow down to Australia and the whole bed of horseradish has to be dug up and stored every year or else it goes wild and woolly-tasting.

Have you ever wondered why Roman emperors were always depicted wearing a wreath of IVY? Apparently it was supposed to prevent baldness. (So does the juice of stinging nettles combed through the hair.) It could also cure corns if you bound the vinegar-soaked leaves over the offending parts; a proper head-to-toe herb.

LAVENDER is a favourite plant; there are not many gardens without at least one bush. There is a Bible reference for this plant too; the Authorised Version of Mark 14: 3 reads:

> There came a woman having an alabaster
> cruse of ointment of spikenard, very costly,
> and she brake the cruse and poured it over
> his head.

A wonderful piece of etymological detective work reveals that *Nardus strictus* was apparently an ancient name for lavender, thus 'ointment of spikenard' was the perfume of spikes of nard – lavender flowers. The plant seems to grow well in different climates; the purple lavender fields under the hot blue Provençal sky are justifiably famous, but it grows equally well under East Anglian skies – which are more often than not chillingly grey. Lions and tigers are not normally found in either Provence or Norfolk, but if they were they would probably be extremely docile; lavender is reported to have this effect on the said felines.

LETTUCE was considered a herb with soporific properties, but only when pounded into a paste and applied to the soles of the feet. It does in fact contain tiny quantities of laudanum (related to morphia) and can therefore keep tame rabbits very docile, and send pigs to sleep! The LILY is the symbol of purity, especially the wonderful Madonna Lily (*Lilium candidum*) which, it is said, can be grown only by a good woman. The roots of LILY OF THE VALLEY (*Convalleria majalis*, aka Liriconfancy and Our Lady's Tears) contain a medicinal property for cardiac disorders, similar to digitalis. Country people believe the plant is the 'wife' of Solomon's Seal (*Polygonatum*) and that they should be grown together. Certainly they both like to be in the shelter of large trees, preferably oak.

M is for MARIGOLD, the ancient holy flower of Indian Buddhists; Mahatma Gandhi's funeral pyre was covered with these bright flowers. But in Europe in the sixteenth-century marigold flowers were used for bridal garlands; in the seventeenth-century the petals were mixed with honey to make 'comfits' or sweets (said to be very good for lifting the spirits) and rubbed on wasp stings to alleviate the pain. M is also for MARJORAM, which apparently has a number of uses: to cure the bite of an adder, draw out thorns and splinters, keep away fleas and quieten a rumbling tummy.

MILFOIL (*Achillea millefolium*) also rejoices in a number of other names which give clues to its use: Sanguinary, Staunchgrass, Soldier's Woundwort, Bloodwort, Nosebleed and, more commonly, Yarrow. The Latin name is said to derive from Achilles (who was Greek!) who used the plant to staunch the wounds of his soldiers. The name 'Nosebleed' may refer to sixteenth-century herbalist, Gerard, who advocated a cure for headaches using yarrow:

> if the leaves being put into the nose do
> cause it to bleed thus taking away the
> megrims.

It was eaten at weddings – to ensure the bride and groom would love each other for at least seven years. (What happened after that?) If tied to a cradle it would protect a baby from being snatched away by bad fairies, and it is also said to grow well in churchyards as a reproach to the dead, who would not be there if they had taken their yarrow broth every day while still alive!

MINT is a feral plant if ever there was one. It is not content to stay quietly in the herb garden but goes root wandering across the grass, under the path, under the fence . . . popping up wherever there is a space in the herbaceous border – either yours or your neighbour's. There are many different varieties of minty scents-Pennyroyal (which is the worst of the wanderers), Peppermint, Spearmint (this is supposed to prevent milk from curdling – useful in the days before fridges), Applemint, Lemon-mint, Eau-de-cologne-mint – they all have their distinctive fragrances. Legend tells us that mint should never be cut with iron – it damages the iron! The Greeks refused to allow their soldiers to have peppermint because it was thought to 'inflame desire' and therefore distract them from their soldierly duties.

Certainly catmint inflames my cats – to the extent that I cannot grow it. I have tried several times but no sooner does the poor plant put up a leaf or three than the cats pounce on it, roll with it, nibble and dribble on it, till it gives up in despair. My big Persian cat (alas, now no more) also adored ordinary garden mint, especially in the form of mint teabags. He would hoick one out of my mug when my back was turned, then drool and slobber and rub his nose all over it until it became a soggy green mess plastered round his whiskers; 'plastered' being an appropriate word! Mint seemed to be a potent drug for the poor animal; for the rest of the day he would wander around dizzily 'high' and even more daft than usual. My friend Mary F. (of 'Snowdrop Dragon' fame) tells how one of her cats will at times sit on someone's lap with its nose only millimetres away from the human mouth. Very disconcerting, apparently, to have a pussycat nose woffling interestedly around one's face, and why does Cat do this only sometimes and not others? The answer lies in peppermint-flavoured toothpaste!

NETTLE, although strictly speaking a horridness weed, was thought nonetheless to have a number of uses. Apart from making soup, and using its juice as a cure for baldness, you could also throw it on the fire to ward off bad spirits, thunder and lightning. Nettle oil was used in lamps before paraffin, and to curdle milk in place of rennet (good, therefore, for vegetarian cheeses). A branch of nettle was hung in the larder to deter flies (my mother used a bunch of mint for this), and near the beehives it deterred frogs, although I can't think why this was thought to be necessary.

P is for PARSLEY, popular in the kitchen for garnish and sauces for fish, scrambled eggs, cream cheese, boiled potatoes and other root vegetables, baked beans and stuffings. It is chock-full of minerals and vitamins; it can sweeten the breath after eating too much onion or garlic, and settle the stomach after eating too much anything (Peter Rabbit went in search of parsley after having stuffed himself in Mr McGregor's garden). The Greeks, though, twisted it into funeral wreaths and sowed it over the graves of battle-slain heroes. Its seeds take for ever to germinate – giving rise to various legends about the Devil taking three-quarters of it, or the Cornish legend that it grows well only if the Missus is boss. Funny – I can't seem to grow it at all . . .

ROSEMARY is associated with many legends and traditions and has been put to a hundred uses; it has a long and honourable history, and is mentioned in herbals from the eleventh century onwards. For example, extracts from the Countess of Hainult's *Boke*, sent to her daughter Queen Phillippa (wife of Edward III):

> The leves laide under the hede whanne a
> man slepes it doth away evill spirites and
> suffereth him not to dreme foule dreams
> ne to be afeared. But he must be out of
> dedely sinne, for it is an holy herbe . . .

and also:

> it passeth not commonly in height the
> height of Christ while he was on earth, and
> after thirty-three yeares groweth thicker
> but not taller.

From Bancke's *Herbal* of 1525 we have:

> If thy legges be blowen with goute, boyle
> the leaves in water and bind them in a
> linen cloth about thy legges and it shall do
> thee much goode.

Thomas More, who grew rosemary all over the walls of his garden in Chelsea, said:

> The Timber thereof turn to Coales and rub
> thy teethe thereof and it shall keep them
> from evill.

It was used at both weddings and funerals; the poet Robert Herrick wrote:

> Grow for two ends, it matters not at all
> Be't for my bridal or my buriall.

The wood was used for making musical instruments, carpenter's rules, combs and boxes; and a box of rosemary-wood was considered, even up to Victorian times, to be the right place to keep souvenirs, love letters and other sentimental bits and pieces. After all, as Ophelia reminds us: 'There's Rosemary – that's for remembrance.'

The ancient Greeks took this literally, and students wore rosemary in their hair at examination time! But perhaps this was also because it was thought that rosemary could cure headaches, as well as coughs, colds, palsy and falling sickness; indeed it was valued for pesticide and disinfectant purposes. Along with rue, it forms an essential ingredient of the nosegays given to the Old Bailey judges – in former times to protect them from gaol fever. Its name is said to derive from the Latin *Ros Marinus* or Dew of the Sea – referring either to the silvery underside of its leaves or its favourite habitat on the edge of the Mediterranean. It has been said that early sailors could steer their way home on dark starless nights by the scent of the rosemary wafting from the hillsides, which sounds more poetic than practicable to me.

However, country folk, ignorant of the Latin, interpreted the name as Mary's Rose and told of how, on the flight to Egypt, the Holy Family rested under a rosemary bush and Mary spread her blue cloak over it, after which its white flowers became, and remained, blue. Other legends refer to its growing: it should never be bought for oneself, but always given as a gift, and when you move house (especially if you move into a new house after a wedding) always take a sprig of rosemary as a happy memory of your old home. The next time you have roast-lamb-with-rosemary, you will, I hope, view those little herby bits with some awe!

Mindful of Ophelia's speech, I grew RUE next to the rosemary. It grew particularly well, which worried me not a little because there is an old saying that no rue flourished 'like that what had been stolen'! Shakespeare also said it was the 'sour herb of grace', its name conjuring up images of repentance and compassion. Sixteenth-century medicinal uses for rue included: stopping nosebleeds, counteracting poisons, killing fleas, lice and 'other pestilences', curing croup in children and roup, a respiratory disease in chickens. Modern medicine uses the active ingredient, rutin, to treat high blood pressure, but unwary use can cause some alarming symptoms. Its blue-green leaves are very pretty, and much loved for flower arrangements, but it can cause a long-lasting and uncomfortable skin rash – as I know from experience.

SAGE was thought to be a symbol of domestic virtue, and like parsley only flourished where the Missus was Master or where the Master was in good health (presumably because the Missus knew what was best for him). Grow it among your cabbages; it will protect them from the white butterfly.

V is for VALERIAN (having omitted Tansy, but not Tarragon – see Wormwood) a wonderful weed which loves to grow on walls. Its chief virtue lies in its attraction for cats and rats – it has been whispered that the secret of the Pied Piper's success was not due to the tunes he played on his pipe but the valerian he carried in his pocket! The feral VIOLET is also mentioned in some herbals as being good for making into love potions, cheer-you-up sweets and a cure for drunkenness.

WORMWOOD (*Artemisia absinthium*) associated with gall (which is either the bitter liquid produced in your liver and stored in the gall-bladder, or the small round growth found on oak-trees) has suggestions of something most unpleasant; Dickensian purges come to mind, or hellish horridnesses to be suffered for wrong-doing . . . But it is actually a quite attractive plant, related to tarragon and part of the genus *Artemisia*, named after the Greek goddess Artemis, who imparted the knowledge that wormwood was beneficial for the digestion in spite of (or because of) its rather bitter taste. A delightful use of it was its inclusion in ink – to discourage mice from eating important documents, and children from sucking the nibs of their pens!

14

❋ ❋ ❋ ❋

PUTTING THE GARDEN TO BED

Nearly all gardeners – however enthusiastic and hard-working – welcome the winter. Those who have to fit their hobby into the evenings and weekends of a busy working life resign themselves from October to February to bidding farewell to the garden at 4.30pm on Sunday afternoons until 8.00am the following Saturday. The garden has to carry on its secret winter life without their knowledge and consent. Those of us whose working week is more flexible or home-based can pop out every now and then to see how things are growing, but the British winter, alternating as it does between damp grey gloom and nose-nipping cold, does not encourage forays into garden activity – at least for the less-than-totally-dedicated amateur.

By the time winter sets in, well-organised gardeners will have sorted and tidied the borders, planted spring bulbs, taken seeds and cuttings, potted up herbs for the kitchen window-sill, covered or otherwise cossetted the tender perennials, brought tubs and pots indoors, cut the lawn for the last time, and cleaned and oiled the mower, shears, spade, fork and other garden implements.

Those with sizeable vegetable plots will also have picked and preserved the last of the beans and peas, planted out the winter crop of cabbages, sprouts and broccoli, and lifted and stored the root vegetables, including the parsnips once they have had a frost on them. My uncle would have tenderly stored his prize Spanish onions in aunt's old stockings: an onion in the toe, then a knot, then another onion, another knot . . . until the whole lot could be strung up in the shed like Christmas-come-early.

All this activity to ensure that 'all is safely gathered in' should be completed, please, by the middle of November. Actually we usually sing that at Harvest Festival in September, which may be all right for the chilly north, but here in the south there is usually another couple of month's worth of gathering in to be done ' 'ere the winter storms begin'.

So organised gardeners give themselves plenty of time to check on the pots of hyacinths for Christmas, prettily arrange the indoor plants, make table decorations of holly and other evergreens, sort and file their garden magazines and generally make the less industrious of us feel completely inadequate.

My father, great and good gardener as he was, did most of the above in order to truly enjoy the winter. 'There is a time for everything,' he would say, quoting Ecclesiastes 3: 'for everything its season and for every activity under heaven its time. A time to plant and a time to uproot . . .' And winter, he always added, is the time to draw the curtains against the dark and the cold, poke up the fire and relax down in the armchair with a goodly pot of tea, mother's home-made scones and garden-fruit jam – and the seed catalogues. With their enticing and glorious photospreads of colourful flower displays giving out the inevitable message – you too could have a garden like this – he would plan and ponder, calculate and redesign the garden for the following year.

The sloppy gardeners among us (count me in here) may well settle down to armchair gardening, but with a less than easy conscience and not a few anxieties. Memories of uncleared borders mix with questions such as: are the ties secure on the climbing roses? should we have brought named varieties of daffodils instead of the £3 a bucketload job-lot, which will probably all come up blind? Actually, the cheap and cheerful job-lots I have bought in the past have yielded interesting displays. There were certainly some flowerless patches, but last year, for example, the daffodils all turned out creamy-white, with over half being double varieties. They were also late-flowering, and mixed themselves in with the pink early tulips and feral forget-me-nots to give me a delightfully unplanned and totally undeserved spring border.

One question that bothers me every year is: how to know when to cut the lawn for the last time? I never get that one right. It's either too early, so that the mower gets put-to-bed-cleaned-and-oiled while the mild weather continues into December; the grass gets to be fourteen inches high and rising, and I have to do it all over again on Christmas Eve. Or else I leave the mower all stuck up with grassy bits, waiting for the last cut of all, which never comes because the season turns cold and frosty from October through to March and the grass refuses to grow an inch. Come spring, I then have to submit the messy mower in embarrassment to a professional overhauler, and get told off for my negligence.

Indoors, the house plants are suddenly surprised by an inordinate amount of attention; they quietly got on with growing by themselves during spring, summer and busy autumn, but now they get fed, watered and talked to on a regular basis, trimmed and tidied and moved into what are considered the best spots in the house. Most house plants respond gladly to this treatment and have learnt to make the most of the winter season; a few, however, become rather sulky at too much fuss and seem to prefer the diet of healthy neglect they get for the rest of the year.

Winter is reading time, photo-album time, memory time. In January, dedicated to the two-faced deity Janus, is time to look back over last year's successes and failures and forward perhaps, to pastures new. A new garden is in every respect a secret garden, especially if it is acquired, like ours, at the sleepy end of the year. We first saw it in all its blaze of autumn glory and I promptly fell for its sprawling charm. We spent the first hour of the property-viewing session wandering round the garden with its then owners, talking soil-types and plant preferences, position and drainage, weeds and weather. After which my husband asked: 'Having done the important bit, would you like to see the house now?' And yes, the house was lovely too, so after all the twists and turns and legal undertakings related to house buying we acquired the New Garden – and an old cottage to go with it. We moved in January, with the garden asleep under frost and snow. 'Just as well,' said my pragmatic other half, 'or we would never get the house in order.'

But in between helping to unpack seemingly endless piles of boxes and find homes for their contents, put up shelves and sort out what went in what cupboard, paint walls and put up curtains, I took the occasional quick sortie out into the garden . . . to find winter-flowering jasmine all over the back fence; a witch hazel (*Hamamelis mollis*) fluttering its little snippets of yellow flowers; snowdrops pushing up thick clusters of green spears (oh good, no Snowdrop Dragon). I was reminded of Mistress Mary in Frances Hodgson Burnet's *The Secret Garden* making tentative forays into the winter garden and being warned not to get dirty: 'I shall not want to go poking about,' she said. But I very much wanted to go poking about, and went out to do some snipping and tidying as a pretext for trying to persuade the garden to give up its secrets. It wouldn't of course; it kept itself tightly furled, curled and buttoned up under the frosty cold.

'All in God's good time,' it might have said, 'be patient.' There were some clues in the form of little labels sticking up from bare patches of earth, left by the previous owners, who had been wonderful plantsfolk. But subterranean activity of earthworms and scrabbling of birds would probably have shifted these about, so it would be an interesting piece of detective work come spring and summer to re-allocate them to their rightful plants.

I shall miss my old apple tree, I thought to myself not long after moving in, but I do have a cherry; at the moment dressed in little brown rags of leaves which shiver dryly in the cold. I am looking forward to the transformation scene in May, when it will shake itself out in masses of deep pink or white blossom. Not even Solomon in all his glory; not even the Queen of Sheba; not even Cinderella in her Perrault-inspired eighteenth-century ballgown of billowing French silk is arrayed like a cherry tree in May. I wonder what colour my cherry tree will be?

Except, of course, that it is not my cherry tree, any more than it was my apple tree, or even my garden. We have only the loan of a patch of earth for a short while, to make what we can of it while we have the time and the ability. And then we must pass it on to others, with the hope that they will enjoy what we have done and build their own ideas on our foundations, as we build on others' foundations. And at the end we have to leave it all behind and depart for a very different kind of garden – the King's Garden perhaps, or else an eternity of unavailing struggle against brambles and thistles and nettles and choking bindweed (my personal idea of hell). Whether our transference to eternal Paradise or infinite Wilderness depends on what we have done, or in whom we have believed, has been a matter of some debate in theological circles. Whether too we shall be set to work in a kind of interim purgatorial thicket is also of some concern to certain systems of faith. But we cannot claim ownership of any piece of earth; even the traditional six feet for physical remains is reduced to less than nothing in these crematorial days. I would be quite happy to have my ashes scattered round the roses in the hope that they may flower more profusely for the next season in my memory.

If every season has its time, it also has its glory. I once read a serious article in an erudite gardening magazine, in which a case was put most convincingly – and beautifully illustrated – for leaving the herbaceous borders uncleared for winter. It provided a wonderful excuse for the disorganised, the busy or just plain lazy person. In winter, it was argued, tonal and architectural effects take the place of colour and light; stalks and flower heads, seed heads and leaf shapes provide the foundation for enchanting patterns of frost. This cold stuff outlines to advantage the overall structures and shapes of different plants, shrubs and bushes: ornamental grasses, honesty, teasles and prickly thistles for example, achieve a new and shapely beauty.

This is very true; on a bright blue winter day, hoar-frost scatters stems, twigs and leaf-edges with sparkling needles of white crystal; berries become coated in shiny ice; icing-sugar snow powders vegetation and contrasts beautifully with the black filigree of deciduous trees and the dark winter colour of the evergreens. But such days (certainly in south-east England) are rare, and we are seldom treated to a garden of such wintry delights. More often than not, the landscape is a study in brown; wet and droopy hang the once bright (now unpruned) borders; the glorious autumn fall of leaves turns into a damp and slippery mess; moss spreads itself morosely along the garden paths. All this glooms under a sky piled with grey cloud, like so much grubby washing, with not a scrap of blue to make even the very smallest RN cadet a pair of shorts!

It's time to go indoors and put the kettle on.